"I'd better get along to the house."

"I guess you should." Disappointment filled her head, but he was probably right. It would be rushing things to follow through on the urge to kiss him. It wasn't her way. But there was no stopping the heat flooding her, the longing to feel his mouth on hers. What was going on? She liked to know who she was getting close to, know him better than she knew Josue. But there was no stopping these sensations knocking at her chest. He was wonderful, and gorgeous, and exciting.

"But before I go…" Josue lowered his head close to hers, his lips seeking hers, then covering her mouth gently. Pressing into her, still gently, not demanding.

Mallory was lost. No stepping away from him. "Yeah." She was returning the kiss. Not so gently, but opening under his mouth, tasting those lips that had tantalized her since first meeting him.

Dear Reader,

I love the idea of French doctors, and to bring one to Queenstown, where he meets my helicopter pilot heroine, Mallory, was so much fun. And once he was here, he wasn't getting away.

Josue Bisset has a big heart but is afraid to share it—until he meets Mallory, and she's so irresistible his world starts to tip off center.

Mallory Baine has the perfect life but she's restless for love and a family of her own. All she has to do is convince Josue to put away his bag and stay on with her.

They work as volunteers in search and rescue, which brings them together in stressful moments and in relief when their mission is successful. All they have to do is make their own mission of love and happiness work out.

Enjoy their story.

Cheers,

Sue Mackay

CAPTIVATED BY HER RUNAWAY DOC

—

SUE MacKAY

HARLEQUIN

MEDICAL
ROMANCE

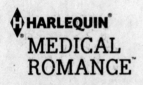

MEDICAL ROMANCE™

Recycling programs
for this product may
not exist in your area.

ISBN-13: 978-1-335-40445-9

Captivated by Her Runaway Doc

Copyright © 2021 by Sue MacKay

For questions and comments about the quality of this book,
please contact us at CustomerService@Harlequin.com.

Harlequin Enterprises ULC
22 Adelaide St. West, 40th Floor
Toronto, Ontario M5H 4E3, Canada
www.Harlequin.com

Printed in U.S.A.

Sue MacKay lives with her husband in New Zealand's beautiful Marlborough Sounds, with the water on her doorstep and the birds and the trees at her back door. It is the perfect setting to indulge her passions of entertaining friends by cooking them sumptuous meals, drinking fabulous wine, going for hill walks or kayaking around the bay—and, of course, writing stories.

Books by Sue MacKay

Harlequin Medical Romance

London Hospital Midwives
A Fling to Steal Her Heart

SOS Docs
Redeeming Her Brooding Surgeon

Baby Miracle in the ER
Surprise Twins for the Surgeon
ER Doc's Forever Gift
The Italian Surgeon's Secret Baby
Take a Chance on the Single Dad
The Nurse's Twin Surprise
Reclaiming Her Army Doc Husband
The Nurse's Secret
The GP's Secret Baby Wish

Visit the Author Profile page
at Harlequin.com for more titles.

This story is dedicated to all my readers,
especially as we cope with this strange time,
where the future is unknown.
You make me happy with your support.

CHAPTER ONE

AT EIGHT FORTY-FIVE Mallory Baine turned up her bumpy drive and huffed a relieved sigh. 'At long last.' A soak in a hot shower, then into PJs and a thick robe to devour the pizza sitting on the seat beside her while she unwound over a crime show on TV along with it.

Except there was a light on in her living room.

And a car parked by the garage.

Her heart lurched. 'Who the hell...?' No one had said they were stopping by tonight. Scanning back for anyone she might've told to make themselves at home, her memory came up blank. Yet it had to be someone who knew she left a spare key in the meter box. Didn't it? *It isn't an uncommon hiding place.* So, who was inside?

Parking next to the gleaming 4WD she didn't recognise, she snatched her phone from the console and shoved out to take a photo of the number plate. Just in case. She'd probably look like a fool when she learned who'd called in but, still, a girl had to be careful, even in Queenstown.

Woof, woof. Shade's 'Happy you're home, Mum' bark. Or it could be her 'I've smelt the pizza' bark. She obviously wasn't concerned about their visitor. Though any of her friends would've let Shade out of her run to go inside with them.

Crossing to her pet, she unlatched the wire gate and rubbed Shade's head, more for her own comfort than Shade's. 'Hey, girl. Who's visiting?'

Wag, wag, lick.

Some of the tension growing between her shoulder blades backed off. Whoever it was couldn't be all bad. Shade was savvy about people, though she was susceptible to meaty bribes. 'Come on inside. We've got someone to check out.'

A suitcase stood on the small porch near the back door and the key was still in the lock. A relieved sigh escaped Mallory. Woo-hoo. Typical Maisie. No warning, no checking if Mallory would be around for the weekend, her best friend would just fly in and hope for the best. She'd been promising a visit for weeks and after today, with their other close friend ending up in hospital, there couldn't be a better time. Mallory picked up the pizza and headed inside, down the short hall, calling out, 'Maisie, I hope you've brought the wine.' There wasn't any in her fridge, likewise much in the way of fresh food. 'Hello? Maisie? That you?'

A cough came from the sitting room. A masculine cough.

Mallory crashed to a stop in the doorway and reached down to hold Shade's collar with her free hand. A man was unfurling his long body from her couch, rubbing his eyes and yawning. Had he been asleep? Tough. More important was, 'Who are you?' she demanded through the pounding in her chest.

He stood tall, his woollen jersey half hitched up one side, the linen trousers creased and rumpled, dark hair falling into dark eyes. 'Hello.'

Hello? That was it? Not likely. Her hand slipped from Shade's collar as she stood tall and straight, eyeballing him directly. He had no right to be here, no matter what he might think. 'What are you doing here? How did you find the key?' she snapped.

'Your brother told me where the key would be and to let myself in if you weren't home. He said you'd be back sometime tonight.'

He looked such a relaxed mess, and sounded so genuine, that her unease backed off a notch, only to be replaced by anger. *This is my house.* Not once had she come home to find a stranger lounging on her couch like he had every right to make himself comfortable. If he was a villain, he wasn't very good at it, lying around as though he had all the time in the world. Though why would someone with evil intent wait in the house with lights on and his vehicle parked in full view? 'I said, who the hell are you?' she snapped, using the anger to cover concerns about not having a clue what was going on.

'Josue Bisset.'

She stared at him. The tension began cranking up tighter. The name meant nothing. Neither did anything he'd said so far make sense. She kept staring at him.

He finally got the idea. 'The doctor about to start work at the local hospital where you're based as a paramedic? I'm going to board in your house until I find an alternative for the short time I'm here?' Doubt was creeping into his accent, and he glanced around the room. Was he looking for an escape route because it was dawning on him he'd screwed up?

He had. Big time. Continuing to watch him, Mallory drew herself even taller, all of one point six metres, and dug for a *don't fool with me* attitude. It came easily. No one did this to her. Her home was her sanctuary, her safe space. 'I don't have a brother.' With his stunned gaze now locked on her, she continued. 'I am not taking in a boarder. And I'm a helicopter pilot, not a paramedic.'

Something foreign escaped from his mouth. *French?* The accent sounded similar to that of the girl from Avignon who worked in the bakery she frequented. 'You mind translating?' she demanded, not ready to play nice. 'Now?'

'I'd better not,' he said. He even smiled. 'It wouldn't translate politely.' He wasn't acting as though he might be on the back foot here and he damned well should be. He was still a stranger who'd walked into her house uninvited, despite what he believed to be a valid reason for doing so.

Beside her, Shade stood straight and firm, her head pointed at their intruder, her muscles tense. But she didn't seem too wary of Josue, more like questioning what was going on. Mallory resisted the urge to pat her because she'd probably relax, and she still knew nothing about this man and why he was in her house. She waited.

'*Désolé.* I thought I'd come to the right address. It's been a long journey from Wellington, crossing over on the ferry and driving all the way down here today.'

That was a helluva distance. Still, 'Don't you use a GPS?'

'I do, and it led me here. I was going to Kayla Johnson's house. Do you know her?'

One of my closest friends. All the air whooshed out of her lungs. Three hours ago, she'd flown out in the rescue helicopter to pick up Kayla from beyond the Cardrona ski field and taken her to the hospital in Dunedin because Queenstown's hospital didn't do major surgeries. Her paramedic friend had two broken legs and was suffering from a severe concussion, having been lucky to avoid a small avalanche from taking her to the bottom of a rocky gully.

When Mallory had held Kayla's hand as she'd been unloaded at the hospital's emergency landing pad, Kayla had been talking gibberish, probably because of the concussion, but she'd said something about a doctor coming from Wellington. Was this man really meant to be staying in her friend's house? Was *she* supposed to go along and let him in because of a few whispered mutterings? It wasn't happening. At least not tonight. Hold on.

'GPSs are usually very accurate with street addresses. Kayla's house is another two hundred metres up the road.'

'Number 142. I have reached my destination,' he said in a monotone as if imitating the voice of his GPS. There was a suspicious glint in his eyes like he was laughing. Yes, his mouth was definitely twitching.

'Number 124. You have not reached your destination.' She retorted in a similar monotone, trying not to glint or twitch. He was beguiling to say the least. Great. Just what she needed at the moment.

'I must've muddled the numbers.'

'I'd say so.' It was getting harder by the minute not to give in to the smile trying to bust out from deep inside now that she was starting to relax. She didn't intend on making him feel too comfortable. Not yet anyway. That'd mean losing the upper hand, if she even had it.

Josue Bisset smiled slowly and easily. 'I'd better take my bags and get out of your way. I've caused enough trouble for one night.' His face softened further, making his mouth even more delectable.

He was probably used to winning over obstinate women. He was built, tall and broad with looks to match. Women would lap up anything he said or did. But surely not a home invasion? Okay, a slight exaggeration now that she understood why he was here, but still. *Still what?* What to do next came to mind. *Nothing.* Let him get on his way and she could take that shower she'd been hankering for over the last hour. But she had yet to explain about Kayla.

Mallory walked through the sitting room to the double doors opening into her kitchen-dining space. 'It's not as straightforward as that.'

With Shade nudging the back of her leg, she dumped the pizza on the bench and opened the pantry. Shade seemed to have decided to ignore Josue, which gave her hope he was all he appeared to be, a friendly, honest man who'd made a genuine mistake. Hopefully Kayla had had him checked out before offering him a room in her house. Hadn't he mentioned her brother?

'I take it you know Dean?' she called over her shoulder, and gasped when she saw Josue had followed her and was looking around the kitchen with something like hope.

He locked a steady gaze on her. 'I worked with him in Wellington.'

Fine. Dean wouldn't have sent him to his sister if he'd had any concerns. She filled Shade's bowl with food and placed it on a mat beside the water bowl. 'There you go, my girl.'

Her uninvited guest now stood with his hip against the kitchen counter, his nose crinkling as he breathed deep while looking at the pizza box. The mouth-watering smell of bacon and cheese and mixed herbs was probably getting to him. It was certainly reminding her how hungry she'd been before she'd seen the light on in here.

He said, 'Dean and I get on very well, and he showed me around some interesting places during my time in the capital.'

It was a reference of sorts, Mallory supposed

as she filled the kettle. It wasn't her place to change the arrangements, except they might not be the same any more. Kayla's parents would be on the road to Dunedin, if they hadn't already arrived, and they'd surely have contacted Dean about what had happened. But then the last thing that would be on Dean's mind would be the doctor moving into his sister's house.

'I know nothing about what you've organised but unfortunately things have changed. Kayla won't be coming home tonight, or for some weeks.' Kayla's parents would insist she stay with them until she was up on her feet again, and who knew how long that would take? 'She and two other people were caught on the edge of an avalanche this afternoon. Fortunately, they all survived but Kayla's injuries are serious. Both legs broken and a severe concussion at the very least. I was part of the team that airlifted her off the mountain earlier. She's now in a hospital in Dunedin.'

Shock filled those steady eyes. 'That's awful. I'm sorry to hear that. Have you heard any more about her condition since you returned to Queenstown?'

'No, but I'm unlikely to until her parents find out more. The paramedic thought Kayla would need surgery on her legs. They were in a bad way. She's going to hate being restricted by casts and crutches.' So much for getting back on track and recharging her energy, which had disappeared since her husband had died. 'Hopefully she'll be fine once she gets past the shock.' Mallory turned away to wipe a hand over her damp cheeks. Life was so unfair to some people. 'She's one of my closest friends.'

A light touch on her shoulder told her she wasn't alone, that Josue understood she was upset. It felt good, and totally out of place. She might have become a little restless with her life, due to not having anyone special to make a future with, but this good-looking Frenchman who claimed he was only here temporarily wasn't going to help one little bit. A short future was not what she intended next time she got involved with a guy. But it would have been good to download after today's drama. Drama he'd added to, she reminded herself.

He must've sensed her tension because he stepped back, putting space between them, not being intrusive. 'I do hope very much she's going to be all right. Maybe Dean's left a message to update me.' He pulled out his phone and shook his head. 'Nothing, but he's probably on his way south and, to be fair, there's no reason why I should be at the top of his list of people to tell.'

She was grateful for his small gesture of understanding and for not overdoing it. It made her feel she wasn't dealing with this completely alone, which was silly as she could talk to Maisie any time. 'I didn't know about you coming to stay, though Kayla did try to tell me something before the medical staff whisked her inside the hospital. She wasn't talking coherently and I'm only guessing it might've been about you.' *Now what?* Did she offer a complete stranger a room for the night? It wasn't in her to kick him out when he was new to town, though he could probably still go along the road to the other house.

'It was a last-minute arrangement after the accommodation I'd organised was withdrawn due to someone else now not leaving.' Doubt was filtering through the exhaustion coming off the man in waves. 'Maybe I should go into town and find a hotel for the night. I don't want to cause any more worries for Kayla or Dean.' Again, he locked his gaze on her. 'Or you. I am very sorry for this.' His apology sounded genuine.

'Don't worry about it.' She was shattered, her brain whirring all over the place. What were the choices? 'It's not up to me to say, but it sounds like there'd be no problem if you want to go to the house.' The guy was dropping on his feet, and obviously hungry by the way he kept glancing at the cooling pizza. Just as well she'd ordered an extra-large one. There went tomorrow's lunch. Shifting the box to the table, she collected plates and paper napkins, and nodded. 'Let's eat. Maybe you should try to get hold of Dean afterwards.'

'I will.' Hope was filling his eyes and lifting his drooping shoulders.

Mallory yawned, no longer able to hold herself upright, her whole body starting to sag with her own share of exhaustion. The need for a hot shower was becoming urgent, which was a normal response after a tricky rescue flight, especially when it involved someone she knew, something that happened quite often as she'd grown up here. Today's trip, flying Kayla to the hospital, had been particularly gruelling. Her friend was barely getting her life back together and then this. Now Mallory just wanted to unwind, but there was a foreigner in her house who needed help. And a lock on the bathroom door in case he wasn't as genuine as she'd begun to think.

Shade was happily chomping her way through her food, the tinny clicks against the bowl as she tongued up dried biscuits loud in the sudden silence. If she wasn't perturbed by their visitor, Mallory believed she was safe. After closing the curtains in the lounge and kitchen-dining area, she flicked on the heat pump that she'd forgotten to pre-set that morning, and said, 'Let's eat before we do anything else.'

Josue pulled out a chair for her. 'You are being so kind. As I said, I'm Josue, from Nice. I'm working at the hospital for two months before going home. I'm also joining the search and rescue outfit. Can I ask your name?' He held out his hand.

She hadn't told him? Of course she hadn't. She'd been too busy asserting herself. Slipping her hand into his to give a friendly shake, she ignored the heat that spilled into her and said, 'Mallory Baine.' She studied his face more deeply and nearly gasped. Talk about being blind before, or perhaps she had been too focused on him as an intruder and not a man, because now she saw good looking didn't begin to describe him.

A strong jawline, a hint of stubble darkening his chin and lower cheeks, generous lips and those big eyes that seemed to miss nothing. Wow. Then what he'd said dropped into her bemused head, and she tugged free of that warm grasp. 'I volunteer for S and R. That's why I was flying tonight.' So this man would be on her patch over the coming weeks. Seemed they had been destined to meet, which shouldn't be an issue, except for the sudden tapping going on under her ribs that wasn't about finding a

stranger in her house, and more about how he
was waking up her stalled libido. It had been a
while since her last fling, and she didn't want
another. These days she was more inclined to
want the whole package. And Josue wasn't
going to be that. Apparently, he was here short
term, while she was looking for someone to
share the bed *and* mow the lawns. Someone to
have a family with.

'We'll be seeing a bit of each other then,' he
replied, unknowingly agreeing with her earlier
thoughts.

The accompanying smile went straight to her
chest, spreading tendrils of warmth throughout
the chill brought on by tiredness and the shock
of finding a stranger in her house. Though she
was getting used to him already. *Tap, tap*, went
her pulse. *Shut up.*

'I guess we will. S and R can be busy.' This
was getting out of hand. She'd met Josue less
than fifteen minutes ago in the oddest situation
and already he had her thinking about him in
ways she didn't usually consider men. Two par-
ticular horrors having hurt her in the past had,
until recently, kept her only wanting the occasional fling. Lately, though, she'd started wanting to find that one person to live with and love
and share everything, even when there wasn't
much time in her hectic life for a relationship,

which was a deliberate ploy to keep her mind *off* what she didn't have and *on* what she did.

When she wasn't working, rescuing or keeping the property up to scratch, she was with her widowed mother at the dementia unit, painting her nails, combing her hair or searching for hidden possessions.

The worst thing Mallory had ever had to do in her life had been to admit her mother into full-time care. It had become necessary when she'd gone for a walk in the middle of the night last winter without a clue where she was. She'd been looking for Mallory's father, the love of her life. Not a safe thing to do under the best of circumstances, and a wake-up call for Mallory about her mother's mental state.

'Have you done search and rescue before?' she asked Josue, more to keep the conversation going than a serious need to learn anything about him.

'*Oui*. In France and then in Wellington. I think it might be physically more challenging in the Wakatipu terrain than anything I've done before.'

'The mountains are tough, the bush as dense as anywhere in the country and the rivers freezing even in summer.' She nodded at her German shepherd now happily curled up on a dog bed. 'Shade works the land searches.'

One brown eye opened at the sound of her name, and Shade thumped her tail.

Josue nodded. 'She has the strong build required to spend hours walking in all sorts of weather and terrain.'

'She loves it.' Opening the box, she nodded at the pizza. 'Help yourself. It won't be very hot now. Do you want me to reheat it?'

'*Merci*. This is good of you. I'm starving. It'll be fine as is. By the time I arrived in Queenstown all I wanted was to get to the house, but I should've stopped to get something to eat. I must've given you a fright, being in your house.' Again, that smile.

'"Fright" was one word for it.'

'What's another?' His smile widened. Used to charming his way through a woman's doubts?

'Disappointment.' Her return smile was tired but cheeky.

One eyebrow rose. 'Disappointment? You felt let down? How did I manage to do that by being inside your house uninvited?' He was still smiling at her.

Mallory surprised herself by laughing. 'I was shocked when I saw the lights on. I wasn't expecting anyone, but when I saw that case on my porch, I hoped my other close friend had decided to surprise me with a visit.' It would've been perfect timing after Kayla's accident.

They'd have talked half the night and convinced each other Kayla would be fine.

'Instead you found a sleepy Frenchman on the couch who'd messed up putting correct directions into his GPS.' He nodded. 'Yes, I can understand your disappointment.' His low laugh went straight to her blood, ramping up the pace and heat. 'At least I didn't scare you into considering doing something dangerous to me.'

'You wouldn't be sitting here munching on pizza if I'd had any serious qualms at all. Instead, Zac would be hauling you down to the police station by the scruff of your neck.'

'Zac?'

'A local policeman who lives around the corner.' The advantage of knowing many people in this town was having their numbers just a touch away. 'I'm thinking we shouldn't bother Dean tonight. Obviously, you can go to Kayla's house, but...' She hesitated. What she was about to say seemed pointless when the other house was a minute away, but Josue was shattered and alone, and she knew from experience how debilitating that could feel. Rapidly squashing unwanted images, she drew a breath and said, 'If you want to doss down here for the night and move along the road tomorrow, you're welcome.' Shade would be more than happy to sleep in her room, just in case she was completely wrong about him.

'Doss?'

'Grab a bed.'

'You'd trust a stranger to stay in your house?'

'If Dean's okay about you staying with Kayla then it's all right with me.' Kayla would've quizzed her brother for hours about this man. She took no risks about her safety. Except today she'd obviously got that wrong, but nothing would've indicated she was about to be knocked out by an avalanche.

Mallory knew about bad luck. Hers had come about because of her choice in men. Jasper had been bad enough, but they'd been teenagers, and she'd had a lot to learn. Whereas she'd been twenty-four when she'd moved in with Hogan, who'd turned out to be a right scrounger who had been enough to make her think twice for a long time about getting caught up with another man. A man she could trust with her heart again.

She did want to take another chance, and sometimes wondered if she was like her parents and would find the right match when she was older. In the meantime, she was cautious in a friendly way. But the restlessness over not having her own family was growing harder to deal with as the months went by. A loving man and kids were all that was missing from her life.

Her gaze went to Josue, who was watching her as he munched pizza. Waiting for her to retract her offer? He looked honest and decent, and there was a twinkle in his eyes when he wasn't yawning. Okay, so she might be too trusting, but better that than always being overly careful. Was Josue wondering how to answer her invitation? Had she put him on the spot somehow? 'Would you prefer to stay here or go along the road to the other house?'

'I'll stay, *merci*. I think you're right. It'll be best to get in touch with Dean tomorrow.'

'That's settled.' Taking a surreptitious look at her guest, she hoped she hadn't gone and done the wrong thing. Fingers crossed he was as decent as he looked.

When Mallory got up to make tea, she glanced down at her overalls. She never wore them inside, and certainly not while she ate dinner, even at her most knackered. She still had her boots on! 'I'll show you the room you'll use and then I'm taking a shower. There's an en suite bathroom attached to your room.'

She'd grown up in this house and still used her original bedroom, which had been enlarged when she'd been a teen. Her dad had died five years ago, which had been the catalyst for her mum starting to become lost in her own little world. Her parents had been so close they'd only functioned 100 per cent when they'd been together. It mightn't have caused the dementia, but her mum had never been the same since the day they'd buried Mallory's dad at the cemetery near Lake Wakatipu.

Mallory knew she'd been a surprise for her parents and, going by the loving atmosphere she'd grown up in, a very welcome one. They'd doted on her, even when she'd messed up big time and become pregnant, then depressed when she'd lost her baby due to an ectopic pregnancy. A stark memory flared of the physical and mental pain of losing her baby, while her boyfriend could only say with relief that they were too young to be parents anyway and that the surgical procedure had not only saved her life but their individual futures.

Her mum and dad had devoted all their time to her until she was back on her feet and then when she'd gone looking for a new career. The nursing course she had enrolled for had no longer been appealing, with thoughts of dealing with other people's pain dragging her down. Her mum had been disappointed as she'd wanted her daughter to follow in her footsteps, but she'd rallied and backed Mallory all the way when she'd decided on flying helicopters and, despite a fear of flying, had been Mallory's first passenger when she'd been allowed to take people up.

Now it was Mallory's turn to give her mother

everything she could, including staying here in Queenstown for the foreseeable future, and spending time with her whenever possible. She'd already turned down with few regrets the dream job of flying rescue choppers in Nelson. Family came first, no matter what.

She led Josue to her parents' old room. 'Anything you want, just shout out.' She turned away. Bring on the shower. Nothing like a long, hot soak to ease the kinks in her back. The wind had been strong on the mountain, and along with the worry over Kayla, the thought of starting another avalanche with the downdraught from the rotors had been high on her mind, even though where she'd flown there had been little chance. Exhaustion always came after the adrenaline rush.

As the water pummelled the ache between her shoulder blades, relief at getting Kayla to safety finally pushed out the negatives, giving her that sense of satisfaction she got after a positive retrieval. Not that her friend would be pleased with where she was right now, but better that than at the bottom of the gulley with tons of snow on top.

As Mallory's body warmed, her mind wandered to the man down the hallway. Josue Bisset. Funny how Josue sounded sexier than Joshua. Softer, as though filled with hidden anticipation. And he was sexy, now that she had time to see him not as a problem but a man who had come to her district to work and help those in trouble out in the wilderness. Tall men with broad shoulders tapering down to narrow hips did it for her every time. Throw in a dazzling smile and vibrant eyes and she was a sucker for trouble.

Unreal how quickly she'd gone from anger to this unexpected curiosity about him. It was as though he was pushing buttons hidden deep inside her, reminding her it was time to have some fun again and to nudge the restlessness aside for a while. But to do that with her intruder? She grinned. That might become his name for his time in Queenstown. The Intruder. A darned sexy, interesting intruder at that. She didn't throw herself at men and yet she felt she wouldn't be averse to spending time with Josue. Then again, maybe not. He wasn't staying here forever, and she was.

Having witnessed her parents' deep love for each other, it was inherent to want the same, and so far she hadn't come close. At thirty-two she was starting to wonder if she'd be waiting till her forties, like her mother. *Not till I'm fifty as dad was, please.* Her family had been close, so special, she dreamed of attaining the same for herself. Sometimes she wondered if she was just hoping for too much. She wanted another chance to have a baby and yet was terrified of a repeat of last time. What if she had another ectopic pregnancy? And what if she couldn't conceive at all?

Hogan had accused her of being ungrateful for what they had, saying she wanted her dreams of love to come true when life wasn't like that. He might've been right, but she wasn't giving up yet. She'd gradually fallen out of love with him and he hadn't taken kindly to that, saying she was selfish. When she'd asked him to leave the flat she'd paid for, he'd left the next day while she was at work, transferring online her savings to his account on the way. So much for trusting him.

The water ran cool. Damn, she'd forgotten to tell Josue not to have a shower while this one was in use. Turning off the shower, she reached for a towel. The system didn't work properly when more than one hot tap was on at a time. She really should get around to having the plumber come by, except it seemed like an expense she didn't need when mostly she was the only one living here. Josue was here for one night. He wouldn't be causing problems with the system much longer.

Josue. She stared into the mirror. What did he see when looking at her? Freckles, green eyes, and wavy hair tied back out of the way for work. He'd seen her in her overalls so did that mean he missed the feminine side she kept out of sight while at work because she didn't want the men treating her any differently? It never bothered her what anyone thought of her appearance in heavy duty boots and sensible clothes for all seasons, but when she wasn't at work there was an array of soft blouses and tight trousers hanging in the wardrobe to relax into, shoes with heels and fashionable boots in bright shades of red and mustard and blue.

At home the hair came down to spill over her shoulders, blonde against the sky-blue satin PJs she was about to put on. They probably wouldn't impress a classy Frenchman. His casual clothes might be messed up, but they were stylish. But again, so what? This was home and she was being herself, sexy Frenchman hanging about or not.

Slipping a thick white robe over the PJs, she unlocked the door and headed to the kitchen to make that tea she'd been hanging out for since pulling up to the house.

Josue pulled on loose sports trousers and a sweatshirt. He hoped Mallory wouldn't mind if he made coffee. Being one of his bad habits from the years studying medicine, it didn't keep him awake. Besides, he was exhausted after the long day travelling and needed a caffeine fix. He'd been so happy about coming to Queenstown he hadn't bothered to stop for a night on the way down the South Island.

The scenery had been stunning, but then mountains always upped his pulse rate. They were magical, and dangerous, and he enjoyed any time spent on one. They were the reason he'd decided to spend the last months of his New Zealand trip down here. Getting more insight into search and rescue in such rugged terrain to take home to use if he found a doctor's position at a skiing location, as he intended, was a bonus.

Looking at the bed, he knew he couldn't go there yet. There was too much going on in his head. Mostly about the woman who'd looked ready to boot him out on his backside when she'd first strode into her house and found him on her couch. She'd been equally shocked and angry, and right away had appeared determined he wasn't going to get the better of her. Not that he'd had any intention of trying to best her. He'd been the one in the wrong.

But, wow, she was something else, standing straight, her eyes fixed on him, her voice strong. Intriguing, to say the least. And gorgeous. Those freckles sprinkled across her cheeks she apparently didn't try to hide under layers of heavy make-up like some women he'd known made him long to kiss her gently. They were like a sign saying there was a wonderful woman behind the stance telling him not to mess with her, and that there was another, softer side to her strength hidden away from prying eyes.

He'd messed up completely on arrival, but who'd have thought both women hid the keys to their houses in the same place? And that they were friends? Even then, he should've realised when he'd walked into the house and seen all those photos hanging on the wall he'd presumed were of Kayla and her parents. He'd been so taken with the love in everyone's faces he hadn't realised Dean was missing in the pictures. Mallory and who he now presumed were her parents looked so happy cuddled together that an old envy had filled his heart.

Growing up in foster homes, he'd never known anything like that. In fact, he often didn't quite believe people who said they were so in love the world was permanently rosy, yet those photos told him different. Love could be real. But was it possible for the likes of him who'd been left on a doorstep at twelve months old?

Gabriel always insisted it was and he had shown him great affection since the day he'd taken Josue under his wing to help sort his life out. At fifteen, Josue had been going off the rails in the direction of a life of crime when the policeman who'd arrested him for theft had given him a talking-to like no other, basically saying he had two choices in life and not to blame anyone else for which path he took.

Gabriel and his wife had taken him in a few months later and had stood by him as he'd fumbled his way out of trouble and into study and work, eventually making it to medical school and into a career the boy whose mother had abandoned had never imagined. The policeman and Brigitte had been the first to love him unconditionally and he had given the same back, warily at first and then with all his being.

But he'd never found that kind of love with a woman. Perhaps because he always backed off before they could reject him, like most other people had in the past. He wasn't counting casual friends. They came and went and that was fine. It was the ones who could have loved him, and hadn't, that had him fearful of being hurt again. Gabriel and Brigitte had been the first to show him unconditional love and he had to learn to return it. Twice he'd started to get close to a woman before fearing they wouldn't give him the love he craved and so he'd run.

Josue hauled air into his lungs and sighed slowly. It was an old story and he really should let it alone—especially now when he was in a wonderful country where he'd been welcomed with open arms and was having a great time. He didn't have to juggle emotions over a relationship because he wasn't getting into one.

Looking around, he sighed. This house wasn't where he was meant to be, wasn't number 142. A simple mistake with no serious consequences. If he had reached the right destination he'd probably still be lying on a couch, snoozing or awake, wondering where his hostess was. At least he had the answer to that question. He'd call Dean tomorrow to find out how his sister was and make sure her house was still available. If not, he'd look for somewhere else, no problem.

He took another glance around. It'd be great to stay here but Mallory wouldn't want him hanging out in her space. She came across as independent and not needing company in the evenings while winter raged outside. Then again, she might be a complete softy on the inside. After all she had given him, a stranger, a bed for the night rather than sending him along the road to a cold, empty house.

He was daydreaming. At the moment he had arrangements in place and wouldn't be changing them on a whim. A fascinating, gorgeous whim, though. Mallory hadn't flinched when she'd found him in her house, hadn't been fearful or stroppy. Not that he'd have wanted to push her good nature. He suspected she'd have had him on the floor with a foot on his back while she phoned the police if she'd had any doubts about why he'd come to be here. How embarrassing to be found in a stranger's home, looking like he was meant to be there, though that was probably what had saved him from having his backside kicked.

Mallory might be small, but she was strong. Not once had her shoulders dropped while sussing him out, her gaze had never wavered, and her tone had pierced him with a warning that he'd better be genuine or watch out.

'Josue,' a gentle, kind voice called from the kitchen, showing yet another side to Mallory. She straightened up from petting Shade as he joined her. 'I'm making tea. You want one?'

He gasped internally. Mallory wore pyjamas, the summer-sky shade making her eyes gleam. They drew him in. Dampness, no doubt from the shower, made her blonde hair darker. It fell in thick waves down her back and over her shoulders to her breasts. Her white robe was tied tightly around a tiny waist. Was this the same woman who'd been wearing shapeless overalls and thick work socks inside heavy boots? This version was feminine and lovely.

His breathing stuttered, as though his lungs

were confused over taking air in or huffing it out. The other version had been gorgeous, but this Mallory? Gasp. Out of this world. His finger and thumb pinched his thigh. Reality returned through a sudden haze of lust. Why had he put the wrong damned number in the GPS? He was in for a sleepless night knowing this woman was in the same house.

'Josue?' Confusion scrunched her face. 'Tea?'

Tea? What? Shaking his head, he finally got his act together. 'Would you mind if I have coffee?' He crossed his fingers. 'As in real coffee?' Glancing over the benches, he smiled. 'It's okay. I see you have some.' Instant coffee was worse than none at all.

'Help yourself.'

'Merci.' Mallory was already treating him as though he fitted right in, moving around him in the small space as she prepared her tea. It made him feel good, like he mattered in a relaxed way. Even though it was casual and not deep and meaningful, that warmed him throughout. It wasn't something he'd had a lot of. None of the foster families he'd been placed with had been so quick to accept him, if they'd ever even got there. Only Gabriel and Brigitte had right from the get-go, and that had been massive as at the time he'd been the worst kind of brat possible. They were the reason he was heading home

after this job, to be there when Gabriel had his heart surgery, to support both of them.

Yet, despite all they'd done for him, the memories remained of how every time he'd met a new family his hopes of being liked and cared about had been dashed. It was as though he had to prove himself every time he met someone, and as a kid he'd turned his anger to hurting others by stealing from them. Gabriel had soon talked sense into him, saying he was hurting himself more than anyone else. It was true, but he'd never quite got over being on edge when he first met someone.

Of course he mattered, as a man and as a doctor. He did believe it, but there was a hole inside that he just couldn't fill. In the two instances when he'd thought he'd come close with women he'd cared for, Colette and Liza, he'd continually questioned his feelings and their reactions to him, eventually leading those relationships to failure. So why was he feeling like he mattered here with this woman in a way he'd not known before? As though he just might be able to find that settled life he craved? It was a foreign sensation. Because she'd shared her pizza? Offered him a room? Or because she wandered around her kitchen as though he'd always been there?

No doubt he was overreacting to her kindness, but a rare warmth was spreading throughout him, surprising and confusing him. Should he be pleased or worried? He obviously wasn't having the same effect on Mallory. Which had to be good, he supposed, if he wanted to get to know her better, as he liked to do with locals wherever he was working. That way he learned more about the area, where best to ski, hike, eat and drink.

Right now he'd like to do all those things with Mallory. Already he knew that? *Oui*, he did, if that's what this unusual sense of anticipation meant. But, like everything he did, if he acted on these sensations waking up his manhood, it would be short term. He knew too well that the itch to move on would strike, as it had done all his life, after going from one foster family to the next, a new school each time, new people to get to know and try to impress.

Gabriel and Brigitte were the people he returned to often and kept in constant contact with when away from Nice. As a teen he'd had his own room in their house, and it was still his. Only with them did he have a complete sense of belonging. There was no family history to hold on to.

The only information he had was that his father had died when he was twelve months old and his mother had never replied to any of the letters he'd written to her as a child. *If she ever got them.* He'd met her briefly when he was fourteen. She had told him she'd started taking drugs soon after he was born and by the time she'd left him, she'd got deeper into the criminal world to feed her habit.

She believed she'd done the right thing by her son and to have visited him at all would have been worse than staying away. After that meeting, she had gone again and not many months later he'd learned she'd died of an overdose.

Mallory brushed past him, steaming mug in hand, as she headed for the lounge.

He was being gloomy. His life had moved on, improved, and there were all sorts of opportunities out there if he let go of the past. Letting the coffee stand, he joined Mallory, settling into a large leather armchair. 'Tell me about flying helicopters. What work do you do?'

A tired smile stretched her mouth wide and lit up her equally tired eyes. 'My full-time job mostly involves flying sightseeing trips up to the snow slopes or around the mountains, out to Milford Sound. Sometimes there are other trips, taking business people to cities up and down the South Island. It keeps me busy, and volunteering for Search and Rescue is an added bonus. My boss is happy for me to help out, but it has to be in my free time.'

Josue could listen to her voice all night. The

Kiwi accent was sharper than European ones, but he liked its clarity, especially mixed with Mallory's softness. *Careful, Jos.* It was strange to be feeling a woman's voice, looks, attitude as warm and encompassing so easily. Could he finally be moving past the doubts that usually blocked him from believing anything was possible? Yet he was still overthinking everything. Though he was feeling more relaxed and comfortable than usual, none of that meant he could suddenly settle into a stable life and always be there for a woman he might fall in love with.

'As an S and R volunteer I also do some of the rescue flights, though I'm only the back-up pilot when others are unable to attend.'

'Like today.'

Her mouth dropped, and she blinked rapidly. 'Yes. Any rescue that involves seriously injured people, or worse, upsets me, and not only when it's someone very close to me.'

He wanted to hug away that pain, but they didn't know each other well enough. She might misinterpret the gesture. 'I understand, but those sentiments are why we do the job in the first place.' Was she completely relaxed with him? *Why question it, Jos? Just accept Mallory for who she appears to be.* His heart softened. Not many people in his past had been so accepting of him so fast. They'd wanted to know his history in other foster homes and schools before they'd asked if he liked eating beef, if they asked anything personal.

As an adult, he still looked for that reaction, and found it hard these days to accept that it was normal curiosity that had people asking questions about his job, family, past. His fault, but another old habit hard to let go. It stopped his expectations getting away from him, and stopped him from even beginning to wonder if he could be a good father if he ever got into a permanent relationship.

The TV remote Mallory had picked up remained still in her hand. 'There's also the adventure of heading out on foot into the bush or up a mountain to look for people who've got into trouble.' She spoke faster, higher, and the spark was back in her gaze.

'You're an adrenaline junkie?'

Now a grin came his way. 'As long as I operate safely and carefully, yes.'

He usually liked quiet women, not ones who attacked the world, but here he was, enjoying Mallory's company a lot. Was he more tired than he realised? Or was this the attraction? 'Remind me not to have an argument with you.' He didn't know if the adrenaline junkie ever took over from the careful, safe woman at the controls.

Her laughter filled the room, and his chest. 'Think I'd toss you out of the chopper?'

'Not a chance. I'm not going for a ride with you.' His grin came automatically, as though he was totally at ease with Mallory. At this realisation, his mouth flattened and he went to pour his coffee, trying to stifle the sudden sense there was a storm coming his way, one that would pick him up and shake out the past, open the gates to hope and something far more foreign—happiness. And stability.

His over-tired mind was playing games with him. He really knew nothing about this woman, and certainly not enough to wipe away everything that had kept him strong and safe over the years. Glancing around, his gaze landed on one of the photos that had caught at his heart earlier. Mallory sitting on the sofa she was on now, with her *maman* and *père* beside her, smiles splitting everyone's faces and love filling their eyes. Did she know how lucky she was? Lucky they had been there for her, had kept her with them and loved her so much?

For once he didn't feel the bitterness that rose when he saw families together like this. The air of confidence clinging to Mallory suggested that her family's love had made her strong and kind; the reasons he was staying here tonight and not along the road in an empty house. Envy touched him before it disappeared into a fragile happiness over being with a woman who demanded nothing of him he wasn't prepared to give. Too early to be thinking that, maybe, but he couldn't deny she was getting under his skin, touching him in a way that was foreign to him, but he still seemed to understand.

Tomorrow he'd wake up and realise he was an idiot and that this was all to do with exhaustion and wishful thinking. Not reality with a kind, sexy woman at the centre.

CHAPTER TWO

MALLORY'S PHONE INTERRUPTED the comfortable silence stretching out between her and Josue as they sat in the sunny conservatory the next morning, drinking coffee. Dean had called him to say he could still use Kayla's house as it would be a while before she was back to something like normal and able to get around the house.

Seeing the incoming number on her screen, she said, 'Uh-oh, looks like you're on your own for the rest of the morning. It's Jamie. He's from Search and Rescue, and Chief Fire Officer here.'

'I'm available if an extra body is required,' Josue told her.

She nodded. 'Hey, Jamie. We got a job to do?'

'Two young lads wandered away from their fathers in the hills near Gibbston nearly two hours ago. They were beside the river. You available?'

Why did the fathers wait so long to call for

help? It was winter and it would be freezing out there. 'Yes.' She glanced at Josue. 'I've got Josue Bisset here. He's going to join S and R. He's done rescue work and is a doctor.'

'Bring him along.' Jamie gave her details of their meeting point. 'See you ASAP.'

'Got it.' She put the phone down. 'Guess learning your way around Kayla's house will have to wait. Jamie wants you on board.'

'Great.' He was already standing.

'Get changed into weatherproof gear. We'll get on the road in five. There's some way to travel to join up with the team. Shade, here, girl. You're going to work.'

Three hours later they were climbing through dense bush, following Shade's lead as she headed higher and closer to the river that was pouring down the ravine. 'Come on, girl. Find them,' Mallory said quietly, so as not to distract the dog, who was a little way ahead of them.

Howl.

Mallory stopped in her tracks. 'Shade?'

Howl.

It was what Mallory had been hoping for. Turning to the man behind her, she fist-pumped the air. 'Shade's found something. Hopefully the boys.' Her heart went out to her four-legged girl. *Please have found them.* Mallory strode out, ducking under low branches, following the rough track through the dense bush.

‘I can hear the river.’ Josue was directly behind her, not faltering in the rugged terrain that was foreign to him. ‘Hopefully the boys haven’t tried to enter it anywhere dangerous.’

‘I doubt it, or Shade wouldn’t have found them.’ No one wanted to find bodies, not even her girl. ‘It sounded like Shade’s happy howl, and, yes—’ she flicked a glance over her shoulder to her search partner ‘—she has happy and sad howls.’ The radio crackled on her belt.

‘Mallory? Did we just hear Shade?’ Jamie, the search leader, asked.

‘You did. Josue and I are making our way to her now.’ She’d given the dog her head when she’d started getting agitated, a sure sign she was onto something. ‘I’ll send coordinates as soon as we know what we’ve got.’ Slipping the radio back on her belt, she called, ‘Shade.’

Woof, woof.

‘Through there.’ Josue veered off track to the right, taking the lead, ignoring the undergrowth, elbowing branches out of his way, turning back to make sure he hadn’t flicked them in her face. *Désolé.*

‘I’m fine.’ She knew not to walk too close behind anyone in the bush. Not even when it was a man with the longest legs filling comfortably fitted black corduroy trousers tucked into trendy hiking boots; trousers that accentuated a tight butt that had her stomach doing loops. They'd automatically been paired up since she'd driven him to the starting point.

Josue broke through into daylight and stopped suddenly. '*Sacré bleu.*'

Mallory banged into the pack on his back. 'Oof. What? Let me see.' Was *sacré bleu* good or bad? She shoved around the man and looked across the riverbank to where Shade stood over two young boys, one prone and the other crying while trying to cuddle his pal. 'Wow.'

She began leaping over the rocks, aiming straight for them, pulling the radio free at the same time. 'Jamie, we've found them. Sending coordinates now.' As team leader he'd call the rest of the searchers, and soon everyone would be here to ascertain the situation. Glancing around, she knew it would be safe to bring in the rescue chopper to hover and lower the stretcher. Because of the proximity of the bush the helicopter wouldn't be landing on the narrow stretch of rocks. She'd call Scott, today's rescue pilot, shortly and give him the necessary details but first the boys needed attention. She wasn't even thinking the prostrate boy mightn't be alive. It wasn't an option.

Josue was already kneeling beside the boys

and reaching for the inert one. 'Hello, Timmy and Morgan, we've been looking for you two. I'm Josue, a doctor, and this is Shade. She found you first. And this is Mallory. Shade's her dog.'

Mallory rubbed Shade's head. 'Well done, girl.' Turning to the boys, she added her bit. 'I am so happy to see you two.' The one holding his friend was shivering violently and his little face was white in contrast with blue lips. He didn't talk, just stared at them, eyes wide, breathing rapid and shallow, tears streaking down his cheeks.

Josue said, 'I've got this little man. He's barely conscious, by the look of things. Can you look after the other?'

'Yes.' She reached out to the lad. 'Your clothes are wet.' Saturated. She'd have to get him out of them and wrapped up in a thermal blanket. 'Have you been in the river?'

He nodded once. Then pointed to the nearby edge where the water was flowing slower than out in the middle.

They'd been lucky. 'Are you Timmy?'

He gave a slow headshake from side to side.

'So you're Morgan. What were you doing in the river?'

'Timmy fell on the rocks.'

'And you rescued him. What a great friend you are. That's wonderful.' These two had wandered off while their dads had been making a fire to cook a barbecue and had presumably got lost. That'd be frightening for youngsters, and even for adults inexperienced in the bush.

'He appears hypothermic,' Josue said after a quick glance their way. 'This boy is, too, though he's not wet through like your lad.'

Midwinter in the lower mountains, sunny it may be, but these kids were scared and small so it wouldn't have taken much time to lose body temperature, and they'd been missing for nearly five hours. Mallory leaned close to Josue and pulled the thermal blankets out of the pack he wore. 'Hopefully that's all they're suffering,'

'This boy's got a head wound, and he's not responding to stimulus, though that's possibly due to the hypothermia.' Josue opened the thermal blanket she'd handed over.

'Morgan, I need to check a few things about you. Can you feel it when I touch your hands?' Mallory asked quietly.

Another nod. 'Where's Dad?'

'He's waiting for you at the place where you were going to have a picnic.' She prodded his feet after removing his shoes. 'Feel that?'

He nodded.

Josue said quietly, 'Hello, Timmy. I'm Josue, a doctor. Morgan's right here. You've banged your head but you're going to be all right. I'm going to wrap you in this silver blanket. You'll feel warmer soon.'

More like he wouldn't get any colder, Mallory thought as she tugged at the jeans clinging to her boy like a second skin. Glancing across, she saw Timmy staring at Josue blankly. She nudged Morgan lightly. 'Say something to Timmy so he knows you're here and won't be frightened.'

'Timmy, it's okay. They found us.' Morgan's voice was high and squeaky, but Timmy's eyes opened further.

Pride swelled through Mallory. They had found these two in time. Thanks to Shade more than anyone really, but this was why she did these searches, to bring home the victims of the climate and terrain to their waiting families. Helping people who'd had a run of bad luck gave her a sense of being part of something bigger than herself.

'So,' she said, finally managing to get the jeans off and started to remove Morgan's jacket. 'Are you hurt anywhere?'

He rolled his head slowly from side to side. 'No.'

'That's good. I'm going to check your pulse to see how fast your heart is beating as soon as I've got you all wrapped up. What happened to you?'

'We went for a walk and got lost. We know to follow the river down but it was deep and fast so we stayed on the rocks, hoping Dad would find us. Then Timmy slipped.'

The radio crackled to life. 'Mallory? What have we got?' the incoming pilot asked. 'I'm fifteen minutes away.'

'In a minute,' she muttered as she tugged her jacket off to wrap around Morgan over the thermal blanket for added warmth. The chilly air immediately lifted goose bumps on her skin.

'Okay for them to have water?' she asked Josue. She'd been trained in treating hypothermia, had dealt with it in the past, but Josue was the doctor on the spot. There were water bottles in each of their packs, along with hot chocolate and sandwiches. The warm drink would help the boys' chilled bodies.

'Go ahead.'

Handing over a bottle to Josue for Timmy and one to her little patient, she called Scott and gave him the details he needed. 'See you shortly.'

Josue was talking slowly and quietly to the boys. 'Sip the water, don't gulp or you might cough it back up.' He had Timmy wrapped firmly in the blanket and was fingering the wound on the boy's forehead. 'Did you see Timmy fall, Morgan?' He was studying Timmy's wrist, which Mallory realised was at an odd angle.

The boy pulled a face. 'He was crying and not looking where he was going. He landed on his stomach and then his head banged the rocks. I had to get in the water to push him up. It only came to my ankles but then I slipped and got wet.'

'You're very brave,' Josue said, before turning to her. 'Warming Timmy up is going to cause the pain to return. At least he's a little more alert now so I can give him some ibuprofen.' Josue slipped off the pack and delved into it.

'What about a sling? Or will we be able to keep the arm still by wrapping the blanket tighter around his arm and chest?'

'Let's try wrapping him tight. He needs his whole body in that blanket. How's Morgan's pulse?'

'Low normal,' Mallory told him.

The boy stared at her. 'Why's Dad not here?'

'He's not far away.' Hadn't he heard her answer earlier? Or had he, too, banged his head? She ran her hands over his skull and found no damage.

'I want him now.'

'We're going to get you out of here very soon.' The boys were approximately four kilometres in a direct line from their picnic spot but would've covered a lot more zigzagging through the bush. The fathers had searched for them before calling in help and returning to the spot they'd started out from in case the boys returned of their own accord. That would've been hard for the dads, but sensible. Once the search teams had set out, they'd wanted to go with them, so a police officer had remained with them to keep either man from dashing into the bush to look for the boys and getting lost himself. 'Have you ever been in a helicopter?'

'No-o.'

'Well, guess what? You and Timmy are going to have a ride in one soon. Isn't that cool? Helicopters are so much fun.'

'Will Dad be in it?'

'There won't be a lot of spare room with you two, the pilot and Josue inside.'

'I want Dad to come with me.'

She gave Morgan a hug. 'I know you do. Now he knows we've found you he can meet you at the airport when the helicopter lands.'

Josue said, 'His voice isn't as slurred now, which is a good sign.'

Mallory dug out the flask of hot chocolate and poured Morgan a drink. 'Have you been in the bush before?'

'With Dad. It was scary today.' Morgan was crying now. 'We were having fun looking for weka birds, then we couldn't find our way back. We heard lots of awful noises.'

'Next time, if you get lost, stay where you are. That makes it easier for us to find you.'

'How?'

'We wouldn't have to walk so far in so many different directions. If not for Shade, we'd still be looking now.'

The sound of twigs snapping announced the arrival of Jamie and Zac, followed shortly after by the rest of the crew, relief the only expression on everyone's face. A good result all round.

'I've called Base. Scott's on the way,' Jamie told them, not realising Mallory had been talking to the pilot. 'Josue, you're to go with the boys. There'll be an ambulance waiting with a paramedic at the airport, and Scott will give you a lift to where you're staying or to join the rest of us for a beer when we get out.' There was nothing more they could do now until the helicopter arrived.

Josue glanced her way, disappointment in his eyes. Why? Did he like hiking in this terrain that much? 'You can let yourself into my house again, if that's what you want.' She smiled now the stress of the search had slipped away. 'It's not as if you don't know where I keep the spare key.'

'I do.' A return smile came her way, making her all warm and happy.

A smile did that? Showed how good those smiles were. Or how quiet her life had become lately. 'Your gear's still there. You haven't had time to go grocery shopping either.' It sounded as though she was trying to convince him to stay another night. Was she? He couldn't stay for ever and Kayla would prefer someone was in her house while she was away.

There was confusion in his expression, probably because of how she'd mentioned him going to her house and not Kayla's. *Welcome to the club. I'm confused with myself too. And with you, Josue Bisset.* He intrigued her when it would be simpler to stay clear. Safer, anyway. 'Let's see what time I'm finished with the boys and that beer Jamie mentioned. Are you going to the pub?' he asked.

'I am. It's always good to wind down and talk the talk after a rescue. Otherwise I lie awake half the night, going through everything.'

'But today we had a good result.'

'I still like to go over it all, making sure there was nothing I could've done better.' Yep, she was a perfectionist.

'Do you discuss all this with Shade?' Another smile.

Another nudge in the stomach. 'Shade's usually happy to have a meal and lie down on her bed.' Or in front of the fire at the pub. 'She seems to think she does a perfect job and doesn't need to drag through the details.'

'Go, Shade.'

Hearing her name, Shade wandered over and rubbed her head against Josue's thigh.

Josue ran his hand down her back before returning his attention to Timmy's head wound and the reddened crepe bandage. 'The bleeding appears to have slowed to a trickle. *Merci*.' Then he added, 'I'll wait in town for you, Mallory, if that's all right? I'll hitch a ride with this Scott.'

'No problem. We'll sort you out yet.'

He gave a deep laugh that tightened her skin further than the goose bumps had managed to do. 'No rush.'

How long did he say he was staying in Queenstown? Two months? She should be able to manage some spare time to get to know him better, *if* she followed through on unravelling the puzzle that was Josue, making the most of the sense of excitement he caused in her.

Josue had an unnatural desire to hug Mallory before he climbed into the helicopter. It was almost as though he needed to say, 'See you soon,' because he didn't want to leave her alone to go back on foot to the vehicles they'd arrived in. Another overreaction, but he couldn't seem to stop them. She was lovely inside and out. And apparently a perfectionist.

Hearing her talk about needing to go through the details of a rescue regardless of a good outcome told him how caring and careful she was. As if he hadn't experienced that with her generous offer of a bed last night. She was refreshingly open and honest. Or was he being more open to her than he was used to being with other people he hardly knew? He and Dean had also hit it off straight away, and he'd found himself accepting people more readily than normal since arriving in this country.

Was that what getting away from his home turf had done? Or only Mallory? Had he started to open his eyes and heart to another way of approaching life after leaving France? Had he begun to change while living and working in Wellington, and now, with Mallory, was he beginning to realise it?

Just the thought excited him. If that was right, then he could finally be stepping into the sort of life he'd once dreamed of. A life of love, with a woman to share everything with. Children to give his heart to along with the things he'd missed out on, growing up. A life where he could trust himself with a home *and* a family. *No.* Not children. That was going too far. He knew nothing about being a good father, and he wasn't putting any kids through the hell he'd known growing up.

Laughter reached his ears from outside the chopper. Mallory stood with Jamie and some of the other rescuers, waiting for the aircraft to leave. She *was* special. Which should have him dancing on the spot. Instead his gut was cramped and his chest tight. Not coming from a steady background ultimately meant he wouldn't know how to achieve one for those he loved. Even if that woman was someone like Mallory, who readily accepted him as she saw him, how could she possibly understand his uncertainties?

While searching for the boys, they'd walked through the bush, up and down slopes, slipping in mud, and not once had Mallory checked to see if he was capable of keeping up, and therefore a competent part of the team. She took it for granted he was. When they'd reached the boys, she'd made way for the doctor and hadn't tried to show how competent she was as a first-aider.

Now he got to fly out, while she'd be walking back the way they'd come, though probably on a more direct route. The doctor in him accepted it was his role to go with the boys and he had no intention of arguing. As a man he'd like nothing better than to walk out of the bush with this woman who'd managed to open his heart a little after only knowing her one night.

Her easy acceptance of him in her home last night after she'd got over the shock and her annoyance had blown him away. She hadn't walked up and said welcome, make yourself at home, but she had taken his explanation and had obviously added it to what little she knew about Dean's sister having someone to stay, and had been okay with his presence. He shook his head. Unbelievable. Not because of his past, but because she'd had every right to tell him to leave and sort the problem out himself. He had erred when he'd put in the street number, but if the two women hadn't hidden keys in the same places, surely he would've finally worked out he was in the wrong place?

'Josue, the boys are strapped in and ready to go. You need to strap yourself in, too.' Jamie stood just beyond the opening on the side of the chopper, bringing him back to reality with a clunk.

Reality in that Mallory may be coming up on his radar as special, but he wouldn't be staying on after his months here were up. He had always intended to return to Nice, the place where he belonged even if his roots were vague and a big let-down. New Zealand had given him a visa for two years, but he'd only planned on staying for one, knowing the inability to settle would drive him away sooner rather than later.

Besides, he'd promised to return home for Gabriel's surgery later in the year anyway. 'Onto it. See you shortly.' He reached out to slide the door shut and then focused on the boys in front of him. 'Morgan, are you feeling all right?'

'Why does the helicopter shake so much?'

'That's because the rotors on top are going faster and faster. Soon we'll be off the ground and you won't notice the shaking so much.' He turned to look Timmy over. The boy's eyes were closed again. 'Timmy,' he called quietly.

Timmy opened his eyes and looked around. 'Where's my dad?' he cried.

'Both your dads are heading to the hospital, but we're going to get there quicker. They have to drive all the way.' Hopefully the mothers were already on the way from their homes in town. These little guys were overdue some hugs and loving.

Looking out the window in search of Mallory, he saw her walking into the bush, being swallowed by the thick manuka trees, Shade right on her heels. 'See you soon,' he whispered, before turning back to his charges. 'Hey, Morgan, this is fun, isn't it?'

It was now they'd found the boys and were getting them out to safety. It gave him a thrill and made him happy to have helped. It was one of the best things he'd been doing in this country. He owed Gabriel for convincing him to come here.

'You need to get away and take a long hard look at everything that's happened to you from a distance,' Gabriel had said as he'd driven Josue home from visiting his mother's gravesite for the first time.

'What do you mean?' Josue had asked. 'Nothing would've saved my mother from the drugs but herself, and she obviously hadn't wanted to.' Seeing the grave had raised old emotions that had torn through him like a sharp knife, reminding him of what he'd missed out on.

'Everyone chooses their own path.' Gabriel repeated what he'd said the first time they met. 'It's up to you how you deal with life's obstacles.'

'True. But how would going away change anything?' Josue asked around the bitterness.

'You might find closure. You could see the world through lighter eyes, a calmer mind. You could be so busy enjoying yourself, you'll forget to haul the past along every step of your life.'

'You going to tell me where to go too?'

Gabriel shook his head. 'No, my man, that's entirely up to you.' Then he spoilt it by saying, 'Some place with mountains and not many people where you can be yourself.'

'Next you'll be naming a country.' Josue had laughed then.

'You've always talked about New Zealand.'

'I knew it. You can't help yourself.' Josue stared out the window at the passing traffic, the idea growing as they made their way home.

And here he was—enjoying himself.

'Shade won't be able to walk if you guys keep feeding her like that,' Mallory admonished gently, softness in her heart as she watched her pet lying in front of the large open fire. Shade was a trouper, and today she'd proved yet again just how clever she was at tracking. Now everyone was spoiling her rotten for leading the team to the boys.

'She deserves every steak she gets,' Josue called from the bar, where he was buying another round of beers for the group. Hopefully no more steak for her dog, though. 'She's not exactly overweight.' His French accent seemed stronger in here surrounded by so many Kiwis. Still as sexy, though.

Not that she'd given the doctor, whose black jersey and corduroy trousers covered a body more suited to a basketball player in his prime, a lot of thought this afternoon other than how he worked as a partner in the rescue. He'd known what he was doing, even when the terrain was foreign, though apparently he had done some time helping in searches out of Wellington, which was similar but not as difficult.

He hadn't hesitated at fording freezing creeks or trudging through mud that sucked their boots down and fought letting go. And, yes, she was lying to herself. When he'd gone ahead of her, she'd been fully aware of him as a man. But they'd been in unison about what they were out there for. 'You saying I starve Shade?' She gave him a smile.

'Not after what you fed her last night. Or this morning.'

She'd given Shade an extra meal once she'd heard they were off on a search, as sustenance never went astray when the dog put her heart into finding someone.

Mallory had slept in that morning, which told her how safe she'd felt with Josue in her house, and how much Kayla's accident had affected her. She'd phoned her friend's mother and learned Kayla had had rods implanted in her right leg and that the break in the left one wasn't anywhere near as serious. The concussion was severe and only time would help that. Mallory had passed on her love, explained that Josue had stayed with her last night, and said not to worry about a thing. By the time she'd showered and dressed in trousers and a thick red, angora jersey, Josue had been pacing the kitchen, sipping coffee and talking to Dean on his phone and getting much the same news.

She liked how Josue had put his hand up the moment he'd heard a search was to get under way. He didn't put his needs first, didn't think he should get to the house and unpack rather than go out in the cold and hike through wet bush and mud. He'd also fitted in with everyone immediately when they'd got to the start point. Quietly impressive, came to mind.

He intrigued her with his looks and that accent. She was aware of him whenever he was nearby, which was something she hadn't felt for a long time. Since Hogan. This interest in Josue was different, more grounded in who he might be and how he just got on with whatever was required of him without question, as he had with the boys when they'd found them.

He hadn't expected her to jump at his word. They'd got down to work on the boys together, sharing the jobs, putting Timmy and Morgan before anything else. The past had taught her some painful lessons and yet she barely knew him and couldn't wait to spend time learning more. And getting closer physically? *Why not?* She wasn't disinterested. How could she be when he had her fingertips tingling with only a look?

There was nothing better than occasionally having a good time with a hot man, as long as she'd got to know him a little and felt safe. *Stop.* She didn't have the time for a fling. *Didn't she?* Of course she did. But she wanted more, and that wasn't happening with this guy. This nagging restlessness had come about because she didn't have her family to go home to at the end of the day.

But, in the meantime, what was more important? Looking after the house and grounds, or seeing to her own requirements, as in having fun and meeting a man? Wanting to find the man of her dreams didn't mean celibacy until he came along. Besides, if that didn't happen for another few years, gulp, then she'd be like a dried-up prune.

Josue strode across the room with his hands clutching a load of full glasses.

She couldn't take her eyes off him. Even though she should. He'd pick up on her interest too easily and she didn't need him seeing that. Not until she'd made up her mind—fling or nothing. Nothing was getting more remote by the minute. She tried to concentrate on the men seated around the table, unwinding and telling tall tales as the thought of what the outcome could've been drained out of them. Everyone had been tense, the urgency greater than even the usually high level due to it being two wee lads missing and understanding how desperate their families would've been. Every searcher's nightmare. It was one thing to be out there for an adult who'd had an accident or got lost; a very different story when children were involved.

Placing the drinks on the table without spilling a drop, Josue handed one to Mallory and took the recently vacated seat beside her. 'Bet those boys won't be dashing into the bush again in a hurry.' He stretched his endless legs under the table.

Mallory deliberately looked across the table at Scott to save herself getting redder in the face from sussing those legs for longer than was sensible. But there was no stopping the flush rising in her cheeks. Taking a deep breath, she got on with being friendly while staring at the wet circles left by glasses on the tabletop. 'I doubt their parents will let them out of their bedrooms for a month. They'll want to know exactly where they are every minute.'

'I thought Kiwi parents liked their children to get outside to learn how to manage nature and what it threw at them.'

She glanced at Josue. Shouldn't have. He was laughing softly, teasing her. Turning her cheeks from pink to flaming red. What was it about this man that got her in a flap just looking at him? Good-looking men were a dime a dozen around Queenstown, as they came to ski or partake in extreme sports in droves, so it couldn't be Josue's looks that were rocking her world. Lifting her glass, she took two large mouthfuls and set it back down on the table. 'Is it like that in France?'

'For those lucky enough to have access to the countryside and the mountains.' His face tightened briefly, then he was smiling again. 'I was born in the city, but when I grew up I headed for the mountains as soon as I could afford it. I'd read many books about mountaineers all over the world and I wanted to see what the fascination of mountains was all about. I loved the outside air, the freedom and fewer people being around. There's a certain excitement about just being able to walk a kilometre without meeting anyone else, but I never took to climbing. Didn't have the head required for heights. Staring over cliff edges, knowing I'd have to go back down there, would only turn my gut sour.'

Dipping her head, she smiled. Again. Hell, this man was getting to her. He talked about himself as though he didn't have to prove how great he was all the time, like some of the guys she met through her work did. Sometimes she felt that some of them had to shove out their chests and strut just because she was a female at the chopper controls and therefore in charge of their destiny. As far as she was concerned they needed to get over themselves. 'Anyone would have to be crazy to do that. I'd far rather rely on rotors than my feet in those places. I've airlifted enough injured climbers off mountains to know where I'd prefer to be.'

'I thought you were going to say you don't like heights either and that would've been strange for a pilot.' He was teasing her in the nicest possible way.

'I passed the sanity test for my licence.' She grinned—just in case he was worried she was strange. 'But I agree. There's something special about the outdoors without having to go to extremes, even here where the tourists swamp the place to get a taste of reaching for the limits in as safe an environment as possible.'

'I've been told there're still many areas to go to get away from them, if you're lucky enough to know where they are.'

'Working in the emergency department, you'll meet people who can tell you where to go.' *Keep talking, Josue.* That accent sent warm shivers up and down her spine, and made her shuffle on her chair. Which meant she should shut up with the questions and put a paper bag over her head.

'What about you? Do you get away often?'

'My job takes me all over the district, so I see a lot but from the air, not on the ground, whereas S and R does get me out into country I love, though usually in those circumstances I'm too busy worrying about who we're looking for and not absorbing the countryside. My dad used to take me on overnight hikes to huts and the like when I was younger. I haven't been back to many of them for a long time.'

'Want to show me one or two?' The sizzling smile was again teasing her, sucking her into his aura.

'I guess I can if we've both got free days at the same time.' Would she or wouldn't she try to make certain she did? He was so tempting. This was ridiculous. She never lost her mind over a man so quickly. But she hadn't. Not really. He was hot and gorgeous and great company, but she wasn't going to allow herself to get in deep, knowing he'd pack up and leave well before Christmas.

Anyway, she didn't make rash decisions or actions, didn't ever lose her mind over any man. Since Hogan, she'd become the steady, check-it-out-first kind of girl, even when it came to planning an overnight trip to a town she knew. 'We'd have to do day hikes, not overnight ones.' She wasn't staying alone in a hut with Josue when just sitting here in a group made her blood heat.

'We'll make it happen,' Josue said with a determined nod.

He wanted to spend time with her on hikes? Time up close and personal? Was she warming his skin as much as he was hers? Or was Josue determined to see lots of the district and she was an easy target for a guide? She smiled. What did it matter? She wanted to spend time with him doing anything and everything. Where had the steady, check-it-out-first woman gone? But what was not to like about him? Apart from the fact she couldn't read men any more than she could a book written in Swahili—and that was when she was being cautious. Her track record was short and abysmal. She'd got it so wrong with Hogan and Jasper. Her gaze drifted sideways. She stared at her glass.

All men should be like her dad: honest and gentle. Working in a male environment, she'd met men like that, and some not, but that didn't put her off them. She just didn't always get it right about how their thought processes worked, and expected them to be open and straightforward like her dad had been. Maisie always laughed at that one, saying no woman understood men better than to feed them, love them and let them get on with things.

'I've ordered fries and chicken all round.' Josue spoke loud enough now for everyone to hear.

'No more treats for Shade, please,' she begged. 'I'll have to deal with the bloated stomach for hours to come otherwise.' Leaning back in her chair, Mallory sipped her beer and relaxed. Her legs ached, her head was getting light— beer mixed with the thrill of finding those kids safe—and physical exhaustion was taking over. It was a comfortable sensation, one that came from having done something good with a group of people all in sync.

Plates of hot food arrived, filling the air with delicious fatty, spicy smells that had everyone reaching for the chips and chicken. There was more than enough to go round. Josue obviously understood how ravenous the team got once they relaxed from the hard work of climbing up and down hills and cliffs, of wading through rivers or trekking through thick bush.

'You've gone quiet.' Josue spoke softly.

Nothing unusual in that. 'I'm an observer.' She was seeing too much of those legs again. What would it be like to have them entwined with hers in bed? Jerking her head up, she stared directly into his eyes. Vibrant gold flecks dotted through the dark hazelnut colour. Happy eyes, generous and sensual. Beddable eyes. *Jeepers.*

She was way in over her head. After how many hours? She didn't do this. An occasional casual fling with someone she was mildly attracted to was her lot. The exciting physical package she could manage, but not this gnawing sense of wanting more. The getting close and personal was a worry. Something about Josue suggested a fling with him would not be half-hearted. She sensed he might take over her mind, her feelings and she'd become besotted. *Which would be fine, except he isn't here forever.*

Josue *was* different. He didn't rush to talk over her or push his interests before hers. He was genuinely interested in what she did and thought. More than anything she felt comfortable around him in a close way, almost as she felt with Kayla and Maisie, yet she'd known them most of her life and not just since yesterday. But she didn't want to be best friends with Josue. This need filling her, tightening every nerve ending, had little to do with friendship and everything to do with getting absorbed into his life and opening up hers to let him in. 'Damn it.'

'Problem?'

A great big one. 'Not at all.' Not unless she gave in to the intense feelings gripping her. Straightening her back, swallowing hard, Mallory turned to Josue, and fell into the deep shade looking back at her. She was swimming in treacle, going nowhere fast, and so tempted to dive deeper. Snatching up her glass, she gulped a large mouthful, which promptly went down the wrong way and she had to suffer the indignity of having her back slapped by Beddable Eyes's large, gentle hand. More coughing. Time she went home and had a hot shower, and got comfortable in some softer trousers and a thick jersey. *Huh, a cold shower would be more appropriate.*

Something solid plonked onto her thigh. It couldn't be Josue touching her. There weren't any sparks. Anyway, he wouldn't make such a blatant move. Would he? Her hand found Shade's warm, hard head. 'How's my girl?'

This time soppy brown eyes looked at her, filled with love. How come dogs loved without reservation? Without question? They just gave it out and only asked for some in return. And steak and chips.

'How long have you had her?' Josue asked as he began rubbing Shade's shoulders as though nothing had happened. Perhaps it hadn't for him. He probably looked at women like that all the time.

'I got her from animal rescue eighteen months ago.'

'Guess you're into all sorts of rescues then.'

His smile was soft, kind and making her stomach tighten.

'I couldn't look at those beguiling eyes and walk away. She had me from the get-go.' She'd better not do the same thing with Josue's own beguiling eyes. She'd never leave her mother to deal with the dementia alone. The nurses were wonderful, but she was the only family her mother had.

Shade lifted her head, nudged Mallory's thigh gently.

'Okay, I get it.' Mallory pushed her chair back. 'We'll be back in a minute.'

Outside Mallory shoved her hands in her pockets and stared through the murky air of the car park as she walked slowly after Shade heading for the trees. 'Damn it. I am so attracted to him.' Her lungs expanded, contracted, pushing air through her lips. 'Too attracted.'

She paused, waited for Shade to join her again. 'Do you like Josue?' Her fingers rubbed between Shade's ears. 'You do, don't you?' That didn't make any difference to the situation. She loved Shade to bits but she had no say in this. Kayla would point out she should have some fun. It wouldn't be hard. He was delicious. But there was more to him than the physical traits that had her enthralled. Enough to take a chance and have some fun? She already felt differently about him from other men. She couldn't let that get out of hand. Yet she was reacting to Josue like she wanted to learn more about him in every way.

Shade nudged her, wagging her tail.

'You're ready to go back inside?'

Wag, wag.

I'm not, because I'm reacting very differently to Josue than I've ever done with any man before, which could kick me in the butt.

Taking out her phone, she pressed Maisie's number. 'Hi, have you heard any more about Kayla?'

'Hi to you too.' Maisie laughed. Then got serious. 'I talked to her mum, and she's having a rough day after hours of surgery first thing. They didn't do it last night because the orthopaedic surgeon wasn't available. I'm still getting my head around what's happened.'

'Me too, though I've been on a rescue today so that took care of some of my headspace for a while. Kayla's supposed to be getting her life back together, not having it torn apart by an avalanche.' So unfair. 'You won't believe what else happened last night. I thought you'd come to visit.'

'Sorry, can't at the moment. Too much work on.'

'I figured.'

'So? Who was visiting if not me?'

'A Frenchman. He's a hunk, believe me.' Mallory filled Maisie in on what had happened. 'It's kind of funny really.'

'Might be karma. It's time you met someone interesting, and hot.'

'He's not staying around for long.'

'Then make the most of him while he's in the country.'

'Thanks, pal. I just might, although I—'

'Blah, blah. I'm not listening to your excuses not to have some fun. Anyway, who knows what he might do if he thinks you're the bee's knees.'

'Time I went back inside,' Mallory said. 'You're not helping. See you.' She hung up before Maisie could add any more stupidity to the conversation. So much for downloading and sorting things out with friends.

Where would she be without hers?

CHAPTER THREE

JOSUE CHATTED WITH the remaining guys around the table, glancing across to the main entrance every few minutes. Mallory wouldn't have left unless she'd forgotten he needed a lift, and she was too focused to do that. There was still half a glass of beer at her place by the table that she seemed to have set aside.

An intriguing woman, with a heart of gold, who liked helping people. The way she walked through the bush without hesitation and was very sure about following Shade spoke volumes of her competence in a situation many people would struggle with. The local bush was so dense there was no way of seeing through the trees because of all the undergrowth. Dean had told him a story about a Canadian man who went for an hour's walk behind the motel where he was staying and was found three days later completely disorientated and dehydrated. Nothing Josue had seen since made him think his friend had been exaggerating.

The door swung open. Shade trotted across to the mat in front of the fire and lay down.

Mallory started his way, but stopped to talk to a woman who'd called out to her.

Josue studied her, while pretending to listen to Scott talking about flying to a rescue in Fiordland. Mallory was far more interesting. Her wild, blonde hair had begun escaping from the tight knot it'd been in to flick over her shoulders and touch her cheeks. Colour in her cheeks highlighted her all-seeing eyes. Her lips were full and tempting. *Oh, l'enfer.*

He'd better focus on the conversation going on around him. Safer. Not that he was immune to having fun. A fling didn't hurt if both people were keen. He sighed. It had been a while since he'd finished with the petite nurse in Wellington who he'd had fun with and no regrets when it finished. But that had been a fling without attachments. That might not be possible with Mallory since she already had him in knots just thinking about her.

Though, especially following his previous failed serious relationships, he found it hard to imagine he could find a woman he might fall in love with. It wasn't that he didn't want to find a woman to love and cherish forever. He did. But his mother hadn't loved him enough to get her act together and raise him. And not one person in the foster homes had done anything to prove her wrong. Gabriel and Brigitte loved him, and that was the most wonderful thing that had ever happened to him. But they were special. Could a woman love him, faults and all, forever? And could he give the same back without question? Without doubting every move he made? Unlikely.

'Josue, any problems today?' Jamie moved closer to be heard.

'None at all. Once Shade got wind of the boys it was fairly straightforward, if you don't count the sharp climb and then the drop off the edge to the riverside where the boys were huddled together.' The sense of relief when he'd seen them, Morgan staring at Shade as though she was magic, had been overwhelming. He'd surreptitiously swiped at his face while rushing towards them, only to see Mallory do the same as she'd knelt down beside them too.

The air vibrated around him. Mallory was back, sitting down in the same chair next to him. He'd half expected her to take a seat further away. There'd been something crackling between them earlier and he hadn't been sure she was happy about it. Could be he'd got that wrong. *Hope so.* His skin warmed. If only he could bury his fears, he'd be up for a night with her sometime. If she wanted the same, of course. *Only a night?* Had to be, or a few, but no more. Heading home after this contract would save him if he started getting too close. 'Shade looks happier.'

'Shade always looks happy.' Mallory smiled. 'Though she does a good poor-me act when it's time to be fed. Or when *she* thinks it's time for food.'

He'd like to get a dog but with his track record of moving on from place to place it wouldn't be fair on any pet. It was the same with women. He couldn't guarantee loving someone if it would mean settling in one place forever. He didn't know how to do that, so he'd go with his default and make the most of any opportunities on offer. 'Do you ski?' Maybe they could take a day trip to Coronet Peak together.

'Love it, and snowboarding even more. Like I told you, I grew up around here so it's a foregone conclusion I spend time on the snow whenever possible.'

Josue stretched his legs further under the table.

Mallory's gaze shifted and her breathing rate lifted.

So that was how it went. She was interested. So was he. But he wasn't about to act like a jerk and rush in. But—but he wanted to follow up on this attraction. *Slow down, Jos.* Get to know her better first. For a fling? Something was off-beat here. *Him.* His pulse was racing and it was impossible not to watch as she sipped her beer then pulled a face. 'Would you like something different to drink?'

She blinked, pushed her half-empty glass aside, and nodded. 'I think I'll get a lemonade. I have to drive home yet. Can I get you something?'

Josue was on his feet, reaching for their glasses. 'I'll get this.'

'You got the last round.'

'*Oui.* And I'll get this one. Want something else to eat as well?' She hadn't indulged much in the fries and chicken.

'I'm going to have a burger soon, then I'm heading home for a hot shower and some clean clothes.' Another rapid blink, and she was staring across at Shade.

Clothes? It'll be bedtime by then. Bed. Mallory. Josue mentally slapped his head. He'd seen those fancy PJs she wore. 'What sort of burger?'

'Josue, you don't have to do this.'

He loved the way she said his name. Gravelly, sexy. 'It's a thank-you for last night. Your turn next time if you insist.'

'Next rescue we're on together?'

'I was thinking more along the lines of next time we share a beer at the pub.'

Her grin got him in the gut. Hard. It was genuine, carefree, and with no hidden agenda that he could see, no doubts about him. *Impressionnante.*

He spun around and aimed for the counter, turned back. 'Would you like something stronger if I drive us home?' Home? *Non*, he had somewhere else to put his head down tonight. 'I meant back to your place.'

That grin got wider, and hit harder. She dug into her pocket, then her fingers were doing a number on his palm as she handed her keys over. 'A vodka and lemon, thanks.'

He couldn't say if her dancing fingers had been deliberate, but judging by the rose shade filling Mallory's cheeks they hadn't. Feeling confused, he slid the keys into his pocket and headed for the bar, needing to find air more easily breathed.

Leaning against the counter while waiting for the order, he watched Mallory talking to the guys. She was comfortable with them, but then she worked in a male environment so it would come naturally. As was how she made him feel—like a friend already. Except the sensations tripping though his body weren't those he'd feel for any friend. This was dangerous. He didn't do strong need for a woman beyond sex. Yet he suddenly wanted to know everything about her, what was her favourite breakfast, the colour she liked the most, what side of the bed she preferred. *It couldn't happen.*

Why were his lungs squeezing with disappointment?

There was so much to her. She was tough, hadn't been fazed with the men on the rescue when they'd taken over the heavy lifting of the kids on stretchers, wore dull work clothes that fitted neatly but didn't accentuate her sexy shape, and yet her nails were manicured, her curly hair highlighted with dark blonde streaks and her make-up light and perfect.

When he sat down beside her again, he muttered, 'Impressive.'

She stared at him, wide eyed. 'What is?' Eyes he was coming to know already locked onto him. She seemed to be trying to read his mind, that look boring into his head with the temerity of a power drill.

There was no way that he was going to let her know what he'd been thinking. 'Why did you choose flying for a career?'

She continued to stare at him. 'The freedom, which is at odds with how restrictive flying really is. It's like going on an adventure every day of my life. There are so many factors contributing to the job on hand, weather, terrain, the people I'm with.' She was telling the truth, but not all the truth. He could hear there was more behind her words, in the depth of her eyes that had darkened ever so slightly while she'd been talking, in the sudden stiffness in her body.

Knowing there were things about himself he didn't share, he left it alone. 'You've obviously found your niche.'

A thoughtful expression flitted across her face, disappeared as fast as it had come. 'I think so.'

Again, he wondered more about what she didn't say than her reply. Had she ever left Queenstown to work elsewhere, or was this the only place she'd lived? Why this itch to learn so much about Mallory? It was new to him and, frankly, scary. *So put it aside, enjoy the company. Stop overthinking everything.*

Mallory led the way into her house, saying over her shoulder, 'Josue, you're back to where you were last night.'

That low sexy laugh came across the gap between them, turning her stomach to water. 'Nothing new for me.'

She turned to look at him. 'Meaning?' He was used to finding himself in places he hadn't planned on? If so, quite the opposite of her steady life.

Josue shrugged. 'Nothing.' Then he added, 'I'm not obsessive about making plans and sticking to them.'

Again, unlike her, though not obsessive about keeping her life on track, she was careful and focused. If she'd been more in control when she'd been a teenager, she wouldn't have got pregnant and lost her baby, and been left with the fear of never becoming a mother. She would've been a nurse, not a pilot. No regrets about that one. Flying was the best job out there. But losing her baby had left a hole in her heart she'd never completely filled. He or she would've turned fourteen last month, a teenager finding their way in the world.

Sudden longing for a chance to go back and rectify her mistakes swamped her. She understood it was impossible, that there'd been nothing she could've done to save her baby, but there were moments when the yearning was unavoidable. It still gave her occasional sleepless nights, and a desperate need to stay safe and not fail anyone again.

'Mallory? Where have you gone?' Josue stood in front of her, worry flattening his mouth.

Shaking her head abruptly to banish the sadness, she lifted her face to look at this man who'd arrived into her life without warning and was tilting her so far off her heels it was scary. 'I like knowing where I'm headed and how to get there.'

'You're not just talking about a day trip, are you?'

Her mouth dropped open as she stared at him. He seemed to understand her, or parts of her, that most people weren't aware of, as far as she knew. Again—scary. Only last night she'd found him in her lounge, and even then she hadn't been overly uncomfortable around him. 'Not entirely,' she admitted.

'Come on, let's have coffee.' He took her arm to lead the way to *her* kitchen.

'Tea for me,' she muttered through the thickness in her mouth. 'Shouldn't you be getting along the road to Kayla's house?' *And leaving me alone to get a grip on my emotions.*

'I've got all night.' He was taking over, making their drinks as though he'd been here forever. As though he belonged here.

Strange, right? Certainly not something she was used to, or even encouraged with anyone except her closest friends. This was her sanctuary from the world, a place where she'd always felt loved and cared for. No one hurt her within these walls. But the way Josue fitted in *did* feel good. Almost from the start he'd begun causing her to look beyond her hectic life to see if she could make room for him—for a while.

'Milk with your tea?'

An ordinary, everyday question, and she smiled. 'Please.' And went to close all the curtains. At least today she'd set the heat pump to come on when the sun went down before she'd left for the rescue.

'You okay?' He slid a mug over the counter in front of her when she returned.

'I'm fine.' Locking her gaze on him, she added, 'Truly.'

'Good.' He came around to stand beside her, coffee in hand, and looked at the framed photos of her and her parents on the nearest wall. 'When I saw those last night, I was a little envious of the love glowing between the three of you. Your parents?' Then he took another look. 'Or grandparents?'

A common query. 'Mum and Dad. They married when they were forty and fifty and to their surprise I popped along very soon after.'

'They obviously didn't mind.'

'They adored me. Being an only child, I grew up being treated older than I really was, and that was fine, though often I found I was mentally ahead of my peers. And Kayla and Maisie are like my sisters. We get on so well about most things, so probably better than sisters.'

'You're lucky.'

Yes, she was. There was a hint of sorrow in his voice. He'd also said he felt envious looking at her family pictures. 'You didn't have such a loving childhood?'

'No.' He sipped his coffee, suddenly deep in thought. Then he faced her and said, 'Don't feel sorry for me but I grew up in foster care. When I was fifteen and headed for trouble, I met a police officer who took me under his wing. He saved my butt, and hasn't stopped since.' His smile was wry. 'I'm supposedly grown up now but it's still good to have Gabriel in my life. He's my go-to-for-advice man.'

Mallory tucked her arm through his and hugged him lightly. 'We all need one or two people to download on,' she agreed. 'That must've been hard, growing up in care. Did you get a nice family to live with?' Was the French system similar to the New Zealand one where some kids stayed long term and others moved around a lot?

'There were four families in total and I didn't fit in with any of them.'

Ouch. Not good. In her book, being surrounded by a loving family was the most important aspect of growing up, but then she'd been very lucky and didn't know any other way. 'This cop? You get along with the rest of his family?'

He went quiet for a moment, then put his hand on her shoulder and looked down at her. 'Brigitte, his wife, took me under her wing from the beginning, and wasn't as strict as Gabriel. I loved her for that alone. They never had children so they were very busy with their careers, yet there was always time for me, something I'd been looking for all my life until then. I got lucky with them, though I still struggle with it all after the way those foster families treated me.'

'To be expected.' Standing still, she watched emotions flit across his face: worry, care, tenderness, fear. 'I can't imagine what any of that was like. *Is* like.'

Placing his mug on the bench, Josue tentatively wrapped her into an embrace, his chin resting on the top of her head. 'We're getting along well so quickly. I hadn't expected anything like this.'

'Neither did I,' she whispered, as her heart thumped once, hard. This togetherness warmed her deep inside. A sensation that didn't happen often. Tightening her hold around him, she laid her cheek against him and breathed deeply, inhaling the masculine smell of his body.

Josue's hands were spread across her back, gentle and endearing. His fingertips began tracing small circles, winding her skin tighter and tighter.

Mallory raised her head, looked up at the strong jawline and on to the dark shadowed chin and on to those eyes that saw so much and were watching her with kindness and a sparkle. She drew a wobbly breath.

'I'd better get along to the house.'

'I guess you should.' Disappointment filled her head, but he was probably right. It would be rushing things to follow through on the urge to kiss him. It wasn't her way. But there was no stopping the heat flooding her, the longing to feel his mouth on hers. What was going on? She liked to know who she was getting close to, know him better than she currently knew Josue. But there was no stopping these sensations knocking at her chest. He was wonderful, and gorgeous, and exciting.

'But before I go…' Josue lowered his head close to hers, his lips seeking hers, covering her mouth gently. Pressing into her, still gently, not demanding.

Mallory was lost. No stepping away from him. 'Yeah.' She was returning the kiss. Not so gently, but opening under his mouth, tasting those lips that had tantalised her since first meeting him. Against his chest her breasts tightened, peaking slowly. Her hands tightened against his back, pushing into him, feeling the tight ripple of his muscles under her palms.

She felt the instant Josue lifted his mouth away. *No. Come back.*

'I'll see you tomorrow.' There was a hitch in his voice.

'Okay.' She couldn't say any more through the disappointment engulfing her.

'Just one more,' Josue whispered, his mouth reclaiming hers.

Then he took her face in his hands, and pulled back barely enough to look into her eyes. 'Mallory?'

'Josue.' She nodded, running the tip of her tongue over her bottom lip. Her body melted at the desire filling his gaze, desire that matched her own and that she could feel right to the tips of her toes. Everything was happening fast, and it felt right. This had been coming ever since the night before when she'd come out of the bathroom in her PJs and robe and had seen Josue's eyes light up, sending her body into a flurry of desire. What made one man's reaction to her feel so different from others'? Not that she had loads of experience with men's reactions but enough to know Josue was different towards her. He looked at her as though she was spun gold. He touched her as though he'd never touched a woman before—carefully yet firmly, making her feel sexy.

The ensuing kiss was deeper, filled with passion, more demanding, and she gave back as much as she received from this amazing man. His lips were strong and demanding, soft and pliant, hungry—for her. He was getting to know her through their kiss. Tasting her, touching her mouth as though he could read her through his tongue.

Her hands touched him everywhere, feeling muscles through his shirt, ribs under her palms as she slid her hands from his back to his chest. Her mouth couldn't get enough of Josue's as she tried to return the intensity of his kiss, getting sidetracked by the desire firing throughout her body.

Strong hands were on her waist, raising her onto her toes against his full length. And still his mouth didn't leave hers.

Was this paradise or what? She felt as though she'd found a place she might never want to leave. A man she might not be able to walk away from. Ever. Her mouth froze.

Then cooler air crossed her lips. 'Mallory? Are you all right?'

Josue read her too easily. Or perhaps he didn't, because she couldn't be happier. Or more confused, but confusion wasn't getting

in the way of sharing a wonderful moment—
or more—with this man who seemed to know
how to wake her up so gently she almost had to
pinch herself to see if it was real.

'Do you want me to stop?' he gasped.

He would stop just like that if she said so?
Wow. But it wasn't happening. She couldn't pull
away. Not when her blood was pulsing through
her veins and her head spinning. 'Please don't.'
She raised her mouth to his again, felt him smile
under her lips.

'Merci.' The word was drawn out long and
slow, and did nothing to dampen her longing to
feel his skin under her palms.

Deep down her stomach tightened and heat
poured throughout. Her fingers quivered as
she slipped her hands under his shirt and onto
his back, feeling the tension in his muscles,
the warmth of his skin. Then she forgot what
she was doing as Josue placed his strong, large
hands on her waist again, his palms like rough,
cool satin on her hot skin.

Who was this man who was waking her up
with a reciprocating need pulsing though his
touch to connect with hers? Josue Bisset. French
in his looks, in the way he wore his clothes, in
that divine accent, and now she was starting to
learn French in his touch. *Oui.* She needed him.
Now. Pushing his trousers down those muscu-

lar thighs sent a shiver through her body as her palms grazed his hot skin and tense muscles.

Another shiver followed as her trousers slid down her legs, assisted by those large, strong, hot hands she already recognised. And he never stopped kissing her.

With his hands on her butt, she wound her legs around that incredible body, raised herself higher. Then she was being turned to lean against the wall as she kissed Josue, kissing as though her life depended upon it. Which it did at the moment. This heat, the need filling her veins, the gripping sense of falling off a ledge into a dream—this was what she'd been looking for, for so long. 'Josue,' she whispered around the need filling her mouth as he touched her, filled her and retreated, filled her, retreated, until her mind blanked except for the explosion that erupted throughout her with sensations she'd never known before.

What happened to taking things slowly? Of learning more about Mallory before getting to know her so intimately? Listening to her gentle breathing, Josue tightened his arm around her waist as they lay spooned under the covers on her bed, where she'd led him after their earth-shattering sex in the dining room. It seemed to have come out of nowhere, even when the atmosphere between them had been winding tighter and hotter for hours. He had meant it when he'd said he'd head away to the other house, and seconds later had returned to kissing Mallory instead. Because he'd been unable to stop. He'd had to kiss and taste, again and again. She'd reacted similarly, returning his kisses with a passion that undid any resolve not to get too involved—too soon, at least.

No. He had to remind himself that there could be no involvement other than a fling. He would be leaving soon and that was that. Unless... Unless nothing. Stopping in one place was alien, and to do that in another country that was not his homeland would overstretch his need to fit in. Or it might work perfectly.

Almost from the moment he'd stepped onto the ground in this country he'd had a sense of having found that something he felt had been missing for as long as he could remember. So far, he'd felt more and more at home wherever he'd gone in New Zealand, as though being so far from his previous life had lifted the self-imposed restrictions on his heart, but that still didn't mean he would settle permanently even if he found a reason to stay. Being constant, stable wasn't in his DNA. Only constantly moving around was.

Mallory snuggled that wonderful body even

closer. She was something else. She was strong, focused, and appeared to know what she wanted from life, but underneath that he sensed a need. For what he had no idea, but she intrigued him, and had just blown his socks off with generous and demanding sex. Wild curly hair tickled his face with every breath he took. Those firm backside curves pressed into his groin.

A woman so different from any he'd spent time with. Or was he exaggerating in the heat of the moment? Though the heat was cooling and he still wanted her and liked what he'd experienced with her. Or rather had been stunned by it. Here was a woman he didn't want to roll away from in order to get on with the day, unlike the other women he'd got close to—and he wasn't even close to Mallory. *Yet.*

This new longing to stay put, to find out more about Mallory was taking over his usual safety mechanism of pulling down the blinds on his emotions. She made him feel as though he should let go for once, to try to find out if he really might be able to take a chance on love. *After only knowing her for twenty-four hours?* This was a far cry from when he spent weeks getting to know a woman and constantly looked out for difficulties and found them even if they weren't there. Dread slammed into his mind. This was going too far, too soon. It must never happen, he could not let himself get close. He was returning home soon. *Think, Jos. Back off now.*

But even as he berated himself, he splayed his hand across her stomach, felt the warmth transfer from her to him all down their bodies where they touched and breathed in her scent of sweat and exhaustion and sex.

'Josue?' That sharp accent cut through his meanderings.

'*Oui?*' How could he deny himself this moment?

'*Merci.*' Mallory rolled over in his arms and splayed her leg over him, her knee touching his manhood, awakening him when he'd barely recovered.

Sinking further into the bed, he allowed her to spread across him, smiling freely, without question. Happy. 'Don't thank *me*,' he gulped. Then swallowed. *He was happy?* Yes, incredibly happy. Unusually so. And it was scary. Yet his arms tightened around her.

Mallory lifted away enough to lean on an elbow and fix a gentle gaze on him. 'Problem?'

Oui. Toi. This woman read him too well. He did have a problem. She made him happy without trying, which made her a danger. Looking at her, a wave of sadness rose at the thought of leaving. He swallowed it. She was waiting for an answer, concern starting to fill those beautiful eyes. 'None at all,' he fibbed, then realised it wasn't a complete lie. Everything was perfect if he didn't think about what might happen beyond tonight and into the coming days. Taking her head gently in his hands, he pulled her down for a kiss.

Just a kiss. That went on and on, until their bodies were hot and tight and he was pushing into her as she sat over him, her head tipping back so that crazy mane swung across her shoulders and her fingernails skidded across his nipples, tightening them until he thought he'd explode. Driving into her, holding her waist to keep her with him, Josue forgot everything except Mallory and himself, joining together, coming together, dropping into a bundle of damp limbs and falling into safe oblivion.

CHAPTER FOUR

MALLORY GRINNED TO HERSELF. Her body ached in places she hadn't known existed before, and it had nothing to do with yesterday's search in the rugged hill country. The reason was singing in the shower down the hall.

Something in French that sounded off-key and hilarious because it made no sense to her. She'd nearly done the same when she'd been lathering the soap over her body under pummelling hot water fifteen minutes ago, but her singing would've scared the birds out of the garden where they were currently digging for worms amongst the weeds.

She never sang if anyone was around since her friends always gave her grief about the appalling racket she made, and there was no reason to expect Josue would react any differently. She couldn't be good at everything.

She also hadn't wanted Josue to know how alive she felt this morning. He'd probably bolt for Kayla's house, never to be seen again. But it was true, she felt more cheerful than she did normally. It wasn't unusual for her to bounce out of bed, but this morning she'd been walking on air. What a night. Josue was the man dreams were made of. Good looking, hot, tender and he'd put her first when they'd made love.

More than that, he'd been good with the boys in the bush, kind and caring, medically competent. He'd fitted in with the search team like he'd always been around. He wasn't egotistical. He wanted to be accepted, but didn't try to put it out there that he was clever. Which was all good and well as long as when it came time to finish with him she could do so without getting hurt, and she suspected it mightn't be quite that simple.

There were other men out there who had similar characteristics, but they hadn't pushed her buttons and set her tingling with anticipation. Unable to put her finger on what made him different, special even, the sort of man she'd hoped might be somewhere out there for her, was not a worry at the moment while she was still in the afterglow of a wonderful night. But she knew eventually it would creep in and set her to wondering if she'd made another misjudgement, if Josue would turn out to be all wrong once the glow faded. The only thing she knew for certain was that he wasn't staying around forever, and that was paramount to how, or if, she went about spending more time with him while remaining uninvolved.

Yet here she was, grinning like an idiot. How could she not? Her feet did a little tap dance on the spot. After finally having a shower to wash away the day's grime and the evening's fun, she'd gone to bed and had been joined by Josue, damp from his shower and ready to cuddle her to him as they'd fallen into an exhausted sleep, only to wake and make love again. Spooning together as they'd lain waiting to fall back to sleep once again had been as wonderful as the amazing sex. She'd felt comfortable with Josue, relaxed and carefree.

Hard to believe she'd found him lying uninvited on her couch the night before. The Intruder. A lot could happen in twenty-four hours. For her it had been a lot of fun and excitement. Even the hours spent searching for those boys and the drinks afterwards to wind down had been different, having Josue beside her. A bit like he was meant to be with her, and that she'd finally found someone who understood how she loved to use her skills to help people.

Her stomach was complaining of starvation, grumbling loudly, sending signals of hunger up her throat. Breakfast was urgently required, starting with tea for her, coffee for her guest. Guest? Not really. Another grin spread her mouth wide as she hummed out of tune. 'Bacon and eggs, hash browns and mushrooms.'

'Sounds good to me.'

Mallory leapt out of her skin. 'Don't creep up on me like that.'

'There wasn't any creeping happening.' Josue laughed. 'You were completely absorbed in your thoughts.'

'Always lots going on in my head.' Breathing slowly to still the rapid beating going on in her chest, she turned around to drink in the sight of the man who'd given her such a wonderful night of sex and cuddles and just being with her. She felt small beside him, but not weak or incapable. He didn't take anything away from her, instead he gave of himself for her pleasure and made her feel secure in his arms, made her stronger.

Despite his relaxed manner with people, he appeared to be a solitary man, keeping aspects about himself close, which made sense since he'd spent his childhood in care and not knowing family love as she had. That made it doubtful he'd want to get too involved when he was only here for a short time. Which was good. A couple of months of what they'd started last night? *Yes, please*. She began rising onto her toes, about to tap dance again, then got a grip on herself. Amazing sex or not, this couldn't go on willy-nilly. He'd leave and then what? Another broken heart? Her heels landed hard on the floor. *No, thanks.*

Josue placed a light kiss on her cheek then stepped around her to reach for the coffee. 'What have you got on today?'

Thump. That was her heart hitting the floor bringing her back to the stark reality of the thoughts that were running in her head. Today was a normal Sunday, with the usual chores and routines to get through. 'Grocery shopping, a few hours with Mum, and calling into work to fill in some paperwork for Kayla's flight on Friday night that I was lax about because I was so tired at the time.'

There was a contemplative look on his face as he carefully spooned coffee grains into the plunger.

'Plus the lawn could do with mowing.' Though she'd put that last on the list. Leaving it another week didn't make any difference in winter.

'I'll go along to Kayla's house to get sorted out, and see what I need for meals, and so on.'

Silence fell. Was he waiting for her to suggest he stay here for the next few days—or longer? So they could have more nights like last night? *Oh, yes.* Her hands clenched, loosened.

Why not? Her body was almost humming with anticipation.

Her favourite song suddenly rang loud and clear from the kitchen counter.

Josue blinked, looked around to see where the music was coming from.

Smiling, Mallory picked up her phone, then, seeing the caller ID, her smile dimmed. 'Hi, Megan. Everything all right?' she asked the nurse from the dementia unit as she walked over to the window and stared out at the winter-dulled, overgrown English garden that had been her mother's passion, and obviously wasn't hers.

'Everything's fine. Are you coming in to see Dorothy today?'

'I'll be there later this morning. I couldn't make it yesterday as we had a rescue callout.' The staff didn't usually check on her visits. Something was not quite right. 'What's up?'

'Nothing serious, but can you spare me a few minutes when you get here? We've had to up some of Dorothy's meds and I want to talk to you about that.'

Mallory's stomach tightened. She had thought her mum had been less aware than usual lately. 'I had to remind her who I was on Thursday.'

'You've had to do that before, Mallory.'

'I know. But...' The sound of mugs being placed on the bench reminded her she wasn't alone. 'All right. I'll be there about eleven if that works for you.'

'I'll see you then.' The phone went silent.

Mallory continued staring at the weeds and sad-looking plants in what used to be a picture of colour and shapes in the garden. These days only the sparrows and thrushes were interested in the area. She should get out there and give the garden an overhaul, except what was the point when she'd only let it go again? Her mother wasn't likely to see it again, or, if she did, wouldn't recognise it as what used to be a wonderful, relaxing place to sit in the sun.

'Everything all right?' Josue called from the kitchen.

Her chest rose and fell before she turned. 'Sure. A nurse wants a chat when I go to see Mum later, that's all.' That was information enough.

'Your mother's unwell?'

'Yes.'

'Here's your tea.'

'Thanks.' Talking about Mum wasn't easy since she'd become so quiet, spending hours sitting in her rocking chair, staring at the wall, when she used to be such an exuberant woman who knew so many people. She now barely recognised her daughter. Mallory felt odd having a man in the house making tea while she took that call. It had been a long time since she'd had a man in her life, in her space, like this at all, and this was something personal, almost too personal when she still knew so little about him. 'I'll make the breakfast.'

'You're sad.' Josue was sipping his coffee as he watched her.

Gathering herself together, she gave him a wobbly smile then banged the pan on an element, poured in some oil and dug in the freezer for hash browns. 'My mother has dementia.'

'That lovely lady in the photographs? Mallory, that's awful. How do you cope?'

The next thing she knew she was being hugged tightly against that wide chest she'd often run her fingers over during the night. A kind hug filled with concern. A hug that warmed her heart. The same, yet different from his sexy hugs. 'I just do,' she whispered, snuggling closer. She could get used to this. *Hello, Mallory? He's not staying.*

'You're one tough lady,' Josue said above her head. 'Come on, let's get breakfast done so you can get on with your plans for the day.' His arms fell away.

Leaving her feeling bereft. Which was ridiculous. They didn't know each other well enough that they'd shared everything about themselves. They'd worked well as a team of two on the rescue, they'd had an amazing night that had her wishing for more along with a whole lot of other things, but two days ago they hadn't known the other existed. Last time she'd met a man and fallen for him, it hadn't been so instant, and it still hadn't lasted a year before she'd realised she hadn't loved him and how little they'd had in common after all. So to think she might find something true and meaningful in a couple of days with Josue was strange, and unlikely to work out.

Sighing, she glanced into the kitchen and gasped, dashing across to turn the heat off and cover the pan before the smoke erupted into a flame. 'That was close.' She'd been too easily distracted, first by the phone and then by those strong arms. A timely reminder that she couldn't let Josue distract her from the day-to-day routines, and that he couldn't sneak in and steal her heart, if that's what was happening. Her mother needed her here, focused, not falling for a man who lived on the other side of the world.

'Here, I'll take that outside.' Josue took the pan, holding the lid in place to prevent a fire, and disappeared out the door.

Another pan and another start on breakfast. Oil splashed into the pan as her shaking hands gripped the bottle. Had she really started falling for Josue so fast? If so, she had to put a halt to everything while she still could. That phone call from Megan had been a timely reminder about where her life was—here in Queenstown, spending time with her mum, flying choppers and helping out with Search and Rescue. It could not be about falling in love with a man who wouldn't be able to become a part of her dream.

A familiar nudge on her thigh had her looking down into a pair of soft chocolate eyes. The confusion dominating her thoughts disappeared in a blink. 'Hello, my girl.' She rubbed Shade's head. 'Be patient. I'll feed you in a minute.'

'Is it all right I let her in? She was waiting by the door.'

'Of course it is. She's hungry.' *Like me*, Mallory admitted. She was thinking food, right? She had to be. Nothing else was happening. Not until she'd thought through everything, at least.

'How much?' Josue was holding up a scoop of dog biscuits.

'That's fine.' She nodded.

He poured them into Shade's bowl, then looked around. 'Your smoke alarm didn't go off with that smoke.'

Another thing she hadn't got around to. 'The battery needs changing.'

'Where do you keep them?'

'Second drawer.'

Within a minute the alarm was beeping to show it was back in use.

'Thanks.' Mallory cracked eggs in the pan.

'You should never let that happen. It could have been serious,' Josue warned.

'I know.' She should have dealt with it the moment she'd known the battery was flat, but she hadn't because it had been another exhausting day at work earlier in the week and she'd come home to shower and eat and had fallen asleep on the couch in front of the widescreen TV.

'I thought you said you liked to be in control.'

Drop it, will you? She'd stuffed up but nothing had gone wrong. 'I made a mistake. How do you like your eggs?'

Breakfast was quiet, almost as though neither wanted to say anything else in case they fell out. Except she couldn't see that happening. Or was that wishful thinking? Because she knew how easy it was to get on the wrong side of someone, no matter how wonderful the night before had been. Her last short fling had finished in a disagreement about Shade and how she allowed her dog inside. Pathetic, but real. She put down her knife and fork, picked up her tea and watched Josue over the rim of her mug. She wasn't enjoying the quiet between them. 'Have you talked to Dean again?' He'd rung Josue while they'd been out looking for the boys and the call had been brief.

'Not yet. I'll do that shortly. I'm thinking I'll drop by the hospital later and introduce myself.'

'What about your plans to check out the skiing and tourist hot spots?' At one stage in the pub last night he'd been talking enthusiastically about bungee jumping and paragliding too.

'They'll keep. It's not as though I'll be working seven days a week.' Josue was watching her with a hint of hope reflected in his eyes.

What did he want from her? She wasn't offering for him to carry on staying here. Not after last night. She'd never get him out of her mind then, or her bed. Used to living on her own, she liked her space and the quiet times. Of course, there were plenty of hours when she wished for someone to be here, talking and sharing a meal, but the moments alone were mostly easy for her.

She slumped in her chair and picked up her tea and glanced across at Josue. Hell, he had her in a turmoil, with her mind throwing up questions about what she wanted. What to do about him, when usually if she met a man who interested her, she got on with spending time with him and letting the fling—if it came to that—run its course? Why not let go of all the concerns about her and Josue and just have a great time? It would be great, no doubts at all. He was sexy as. And fun. And interesting. Those three aspects made her wriggle with happiness.

She gave in—a little. 'We could go skiing next weekend, if you like.' She pointed out the window to snow-covered Cecil Peak on the other side of Lake Wakatipu. She never got tired of the stunning winter view, where the mountain appeared to be within arm's reach, the crisp white reflected on the mirror-like lake. Growing up here, the mountains were in her blood. The months she'd spent with Hogan in outback Australia where the view was brown and dry and flat compared to here for as far as the eye could see had made her feel she was on Mars.

'We can go to whichever ski field you'd prefer.'

His smile was devastating. '*Oui*. Coronet Peak first. I'm looking forward to it already.'

First? There'd be other times? Showed what offering to join him on one trip led to. Excitement tripped through her. Leaping up to get away from that smile destroying her need to remain sensible about Josue, Mallory tipped out the cold tea and started making another one. 'Let's hope we don't get called out to a rescue.'

His smile didn't dim a fraction. 'Then we'll do that and go skiing another time.'

Good answer. Except wasn't she supposed to

be drawing back from the temptation that was Josue? The only way to do that was to put some space between them so she could think clearly without distractions like that damned smile. 'Right, guess I'd better get a move on.' *Wasn't I making a mug of tea?* She could drink it while applying her make-up. 'I need to be at the rest home by eleven and there's no such thing as a quick call into work. There're always wannabe pilots hanging around, wanting to talk the rotors off the flying machines.'

'I'll get out of your way,' Josue said. 'See you later?'

It would be so easy to say yes and have another wonderful night. Too easy. Drawing in a deep breath, she told him, 'I'm not sure what time I'll be done with Mum or the other chores I need to do. Maybe another day?' She was consumed with thoughts about what the nurse had to say about her mother. Fingers crossed Mum's placid persona hadn't started changing to something more aggressive, as the doctor and nurses had warned could happen. The last thing imaginable was her mother being aggressive. Not once in her life had Mallory seen her get so angry that she would lose control and hit out verbally or physically, and yet the medics had warned of the possibility.

'Yes, of course.' Josue's smile was gone. The

light in those amazing eyes had flicked off. His relaxed stance had tightened. He started walking away.

Somehow, she'd hurt him. A lot. 'Josue?'

He waved over his shoulder and kept going.

No, damn it. Whatever she'd done had not been with the intention of hurting him. It had been about protecting herself. She caught up to him at the front door. 'Stop, Josue. Last night— well, it was wonderful.'

He nodded.

Now what? Try being honest, whatever that was in this case. 'I have never rushed into bed with a man so fast before. I have no regrets.'

Another nod. He wasn't making this easy.

Did he see her words as rejection? Possibly. It was, in a way, because she was afraid where this might lead. 'It's early days, Josue. We don't know each other very well, though I trust you and like what I've seen so far.' *You can do better than that, Mallory Baine.*

'It's all right, Mallory, I understand.' He ran a finger down her cheek so softly it sent whispers of heat throughout her body.

How was she supposed to walk away from that? 'I don't think you do,' she growled through the longing building up inside. 'I'm not saying no to having anything to do with you, but I need to take things slowly.' Heck, when she got honest there was no stopping her.

Now he smiled. 'Bit late for that, don't you think?'

Warmth broke out, pushing away the chill that had begun creeping over her. 'True.' Where to from here? 'I have a busy life that I can't put on hold all the time. Besides, you're not here for ever, Josue.'

'I'm not usually anywhere for long, Mallory. I move on a lot.' The seriousness in his voice was matching a darkening in his eyes. He was giving her a warning. 'I never stop still for any length of time.'

She should be grateful. It matched the warnings she'd been trying to raise within herself. They could continue having a fling and there'd be no expectations of more to follow. While flings were supposedly short term—her few had been—she already felt deep inside that nothing with Josue would be short term for her. Already she'd seen a sensitive side to him that called to her to share herself, to open up to him about her needs and dreams, and hopefully encourage him to talk about his in return.

'Thank you for your honesty.'

Had she just got herself into a deeper quandary? Nothing was going to be solved while standing here talking awkwardly, so it'd be best to get on with the day and let her mind quietly mull over everything. In the meantime, she smiled, she couldn't just walk away without acknowledging he had affected her, and she did want more. Up on her toes, she kissed his cheek, and said, 'It *was* a wonderful night. But…'

'But what?' Driving away from Mallory had Josue grimacing with reluctance. He'd rather be back in her house, talking and sharing another coffee, making plans for going skiing or staying in and cuddling up in bed with their bodies entwined. Except for the sentence she hadn't finished.

Last night had to be one of the most amazing times he'd experienced with a woman, and that came from the way she made him feel so at home with her—if this unusual sense of having found his niche in the world was anything to go by. Not once had she made him feel out of place. *Wrong.* There had been that moment when he'd been lumbering to his feet from her couch that first night to face her steady glare and demanding questions.

But that had passed quickly and last night she'd been as ready for his kisses as he had hers, then when they'd let down the last barriers and he'd lifted her into his arms and up against the wall she'd been more than ready for him.

'But…' she'd said.

Not once had he questioned what they were doing in terms of what Mallory's expectations might have been. Was this to be a one-night stand? Or the beginning of a fling? A relationship? His stomach pulled inwards. That wasn't happening. They'd both end up hurt if that was her expectation. She'd been happy to share their lovemaking. Not that there'd been time to think about anything once they'd started kissing.

He had hauled on the brakes briefly, worried she would change her mind, but his concern had quickly been doused with more hot kisses followed with opening their bodies to each other. It had happened in a flash of need and heat that had scorched the air around them and blanked everything from his mind except Mallory and what she'd been doing to him.

The house he was making for appeared in his vision within moments. No wonder Mallory had been startled when he'd said where he'd been heading the other night. He had been so close. No regrets, however, or he might not have got to know Mallory so well so quickly. The chances of going out on yesterday's search would've been remote as no one had known he was in town, and even if he had and had ended up at the pub with everyone, he doubted he'd have spent much time with her.

Parking in the driveway he looked around at the neat lawns and tidy gardens. Obviously, Kayla spent more time working on her property than Mallory did, unless she paid to have it done. Everything was in its place, not a blade of grass too long, no weeds had dared raise their green heads between the shrubs, which meant inside would be as immaculate. And impersonal, he sighed.

But, then, he wasn't known for making his apartments anything more than somewhere to put his feet up. It might be why he'd felt oddly comfortable at Mallory's with her photos and shelves of books. It was cosy and friendly. With Shade's basket, rug and toys everything felt warm and homely. As far as he understood homely to be, that was.

At the front door he inserted the key he found in the meter box and let himself in. *Oui*, spick and span, not a dust mote to be seen. Hopefully Kayla had someone come in and do the work or he'd be busier here than at the emergency department. Chuckling as he made his way through the house, he found the bedroom obviously allocated to him with a pile of towels on the dresser and extra pillows stacked neatly on the end of the bed. Everything was too perfect, but he had no complaints. He'd have hated to find the home grubby and unkempt. It was the warmth of Mallory's home, as well Mallory herself, that had him looking twice here.

Get out of my head, Mallory Baine.

Like that was going to work. Not even before last night, and now there wasn't a hope in Hades. At first, she'd tickled his interest, and then she'd exploded into his head and shaken him to the core. Throughout his life he'd looked for love—mostly from foster parents because there hadn't been anyone else to expect it from. He'd made two close friends at medical school, but guys didn't admit that a close friendship had an element of love involved. What he'd presumed love to be with the two women he had got into serious relationships with had fallen by the wayside as he'd fought his demons. He'd wanted to fall in love but conversely had kept questioning himself about whether he'd finally found love, pushing away from both women when he'd begun overthinking his inexperience with emotional commitment. He'd hurt them both, and himself, due to his lack of confidence.

Now he'd met Mallory and the same questions were beginning to haunt him, only there was a difference. Never before had he felt anything near the warmth and sense of belonging he already felt with Mallory.

Which was why you warned her you don't settle down anywhere long term. He'd been looking out for her, didn't want to hurt her at all. Yes, and he'd been thinking of himself because he would not be staying on in New Zealand once his time at Queenstown Hospital was up. Would he be able to walk away from here as per normal when there wasn't a lot to hold him in Nice?

When he'd been preparing to fly out of France, Gabriel had told him to be open to opportunities, to grab them with both hands and see where they led. As if Gabriel believed he should be open-minded to another country, another language and a different lifestyle, and to a wonderful, caring and fun woman who might creep under his skin so fast it would be impossible to understand and accept as what he wanted, and needed.

He wouldn't.

He'd get on with what he'd come here to do, and see Mallory when they crossed paths in work or with Search and Rescue. She'd said she was unavailable tonight, but he didn't believe her. She was putting distance between them and he should be grateful, not feel let down. She was doing what he normally did. It felt as though she had rejected him. He was used to doing the rejecting long before his heart was involved, because that kept him safe. But last night had been wonderful, exciting and heartwarming. If Mallory thought they should take things slowly, then what had last night meant? There'd been no slowing down whatsoever.

Hades, but he really didn't know what he wanted. *Yes, you do.* What he didn't know was what to do about it. Risk-taking was not his thing, and getting close to Mallory would be the biggest risk of all.

One day at a time, *mon ami.*

She'd turned down his suggestion of getting together tonight. Rejection stung. What now? Go slowly, spend time with her whenever possible, take the risk she might turn him down again? Was working here and then returning home to France without getting to know Mallory even a viable option? Or would it be best to spend time with her and take whatever consequences arose on the chin?

One day at a time. It was possible. If he wanted this.

Right now, he had his bags to unpack and a department head to meet.

His phone vibrated in his pocket.

His chest expanded as warmth stole through him. *Mallory?*

Dean's name flashed on the screen.

Josue grunted a laugh at himself. Served him right for getting so excited over a phone ringing. '*Bonjour.* How's everything?'

* * *

'Come in, Shade.' Mallory's mother's eyes lit up as the dog bounded into her room. 'How's our girl?'

Shade laid her head on Dorothy's knees for the customary pat while Mallory placed the caramel chocolate and oranges she'd brought on the table, before giving her mother a kiss and then a hug she didn't want to stop. This was her mum. 'How's things, Mum?' At least she'd remembered Shade's name.

'I can't find my pyjamas anywhere. Did you take them home to wash?'

'No, I didn't. I'll have a look around, shall I?'

'Megan's done that, and she didn't find them. Someone's taken my slippers too.'

Mallory sighed. This wasn't how she liked the day to start off, though to be fair her mum was sounding quite lucid today. Opening drawers and lifting clothes, she searched for any of the three sets of pyjamas usually there and came up blank. They were most likely hidden somewhere in the room, though Megan had said she couldn't find them anywhere when they'd had their talk. This was not an uncommon problem. Her mother often hid items like a pair of earrings or her favourite books and they inevitably turned up behind other books on the shelf, or in the back of a cupboard behind towels or shoes. 'I can't find them either. Let's do your nails now and I'll take another look later.'

Megan had also told her how her mother had started going for walks in the middle of the night. She'd been found in the staff kitchen, and out in the gardens, sitting watching the stars with only a thin dressing gown on in the bitter cold. It wasn't unusual with dementia and the staff had only wanted to keep her up to date with everything, but it had knocked Mallory. Knowing this was coming and actually hearing about her mother's wanderings were two different things and it upset her. There was nothing she could do to prevent her mother from doing this, and had to accept the staff were doing their best to keep her safe.

Mallory sighed and got out the nail polish remover and a bottle of polish before placing a stool by her mum's feet, ready to get on with making her mother happy.

'What colour this week?'

Mallory rubbed the wriggling feet before her to warm them. 'I've got blue with sparkles.'

'Goody. Reminds me of summer skies.'

It was one of her mother's better days. Despite the missing clothes, she was more alert and there hadn't been an awkward moment when she didn't know her daughter. Mallory smiled softly.

Of all the moments of forgetfulness and agitation the one that always got her in the heart was her mum forgetting her daughter's name. Sometimes it was only her name she forgot, other times she didn't even know who Mallory was. Mallory ranked them together. Hard, painful lumps of sorrow always filled her heart and stomach and brought on a load of memories of growing up and being laughed with, growled at, teased and encouraged by her mother's strong yet sweet voice. *Mallory, you mustn't. Mallory, yes, you can go. No, Mallory, don't do that. I love you, Mallory.*

Her heart swelled. She'd had a wonderful childhood that had followed her into adulthood, giving her the grounding for who she'd become and what she'd wanted for the future. Her future had to contain love. Deep and abiding love. She had plenty to give. It wasn't wrong to expect some in return.

Josue popped into her head. They'd clicked from the beginning. Yesterday's rescue showed how well they worked together. Last night in bed they'd been almost one, had read each other like a book. Already she felt he had a place in her life, as though she couldn't let him go. But he'd warned her he didn't settle anywhere for long, so backing off a bit would be wise. She glanced at her mother, who was watching her paint a nail. She wouldn't be leaving Queenstown to follow Josue anywhere. 'I've met a man I like, Mum. He's staying at Kayla's house and going to work at the hospital.'

'Handy for you.' Her mother's smiles were crooked since having some teeth removed, as though she was trying to hide the gaps.

Mallory had arranged an appointment in a few weeks with an orthodontist in Dunedin to sort out getting false teeth for her. 'He's French, from Nice. And he's gorgeous.' She kissed the tips of her fingers on one hand and spread them wide.

'Les Francais s'embrassent comme le diable.'

'What did you just say?' Her mother didn't speak French. Or so she'd believed.

'Frenchmen kiss like devils.' There was a twinkle in her eyes unlike any Mallory had seen in years.

'You know this how?'

'I kissed a Frenchman once. More than once really. When I was nineteen and went to France with my sisters. We met some men at the camping ground we were staying in. I fell in love with him.'

'What happened?' Mallory asked, the nail-polish brush hovering in the air above the middle toe. She'd never known her mother had once gone to France, let alone fallen in love while there. Was this true or a figment of her imagination?

'We had a good time and then I fell out of love and came home.' Her mother's eyes were flooded with memories. Good ones, judging by the soft smile lifting her mouth. A familiar smile she'd seen her mother give her father often throughout her life. It always softened Mallory's heart to know how in love her parents had been in their marriage. And now she was learning there'd been another man her mother might have smiled at like that. A Frenchman to boot.

But her mum had said she'd fallen out of love. *Like I did with Hogan when he started getting too demanding about how I did the housework or drove the car? Could I be more like Mum than I've ever considered?* Hey, that might mean there *was* someone special waiting around the corner like her dad had been for her mother. Josue? But he wasn't around any corner. He'd been in her house, her bed. She'd met him and they got on brilliantly. She was forgetting—or ignoring—the fact he'd be heading away again. Another thought brought reality to the fore. Even if she and Josue did get close enough to want to be together and she was free to follow him to France, she couldn't work. The language barrier would prevent her endorsing her pilot's licence there, so she'd be unemployable except for possibly a mundane job that brought her no excitement. It would be for the same reason she wouldn't be able to qualify as a paramedic either. The last thing she'd ever want to do would be to rely on someone else to support her, even for the time it took her to become fluent in another language—which could take years.

'Mallory, the polish is drying on the brush.'

It was. 'You surprised me about your Frenchman, and I forgot what I was doing.' Definitely one of her mum's better days. Almost how it used to be between them. 'What was his name?'

'Who? Tell me about your man.' Mischief twinkled out of pale blue eyes that had seen a lot over a lifetime of family and hard work, diverting attention from her past love.

'Mum, he's not my man.' And wasn't going to be if she remained sensible. If she decided to be less sensible, then he'd be her lover until he disappeared on a big tin bird and she'd get back to her normal, gratifying life. Alone. But not lonely. She had her friends and mother. Why did that suddenly make her feel despondent? She loved her job and being a part of the Search and Rescue team. Her home was comfortable, though there was always something needing to be done to it. Now that Kayla had returned home and was living almost next door, and Maisie was dealing with her own problems but with the potential of also coming home soon, she was happy.

Except it was time to find a man to settle down with permanently and get rid of this restlessness. Josue didn't fit her needs. He moved on a lot. She stayed put. So her heart would be at stake if she fell for him. She'd been there twice, and wasn't looking for a third mistake.

'Mallory Baine, when you get distracted like that, I know something—or someone—has got you in a dither. Now spill. Who is he?'

Forget losing her memory. This was the version of her mother when Mallory had been a teenager, testing her toes in the world of boys. She laughed. 'Josue, and, yes, he does kiss like the devil.' Too much information probably but she was so enjoying this rare moment with her mother that she didn't care.

'We clicked right from the start when I found him in my house, lying on the couch.' She went on to explain what had happened and how Josue had stayed the night. She didn't mention the next night and why he'd stayed then as well. That was far too much information. Not even at her most understanding would her mother have been hearing that.

'I'm glad you've met this man and you like him so much. It's about time.'

'You're rushing things, Mum.' Which was unlike her. Could it be that she wanted to see her daughter settled while she could still understand what was going on half of the time? Mallory's heart bumped. 'I am not falling in love and about to ride off into the sunset with him.'

If only it was that simple. But then nothing worth having was ever straightforward, or so her parents had repeatedly told her when she'd been growing up. So far, she'd chalked up one pregnancy that had ended disastrously and left her fearful of never having children. The relationship with Jasper, the baby's father, had ended equally badly, as had her relationship with Hogan, which, in hindsight, she'd been glad had run its course.

Career-wise, she had few regrets about not following through with the nursing course she'd signed up for as she'd been about to leave school, despite her having planned on becoming a nurse all her life—until the day her baby had died.

Being a pilot was wonderful and took her to places she'd never otherwise see. It also stretched her courage when flying in turbulent weather or retrieving people from rough seas or off sheer cliffs. It had taught her to be confident but wary, to be vigilant and focused. Now she wouldn't trade her career for any other, but she'd never quite let go of the idea of nursing, because it meant helping people. Being a first-aider was the antidote. In a way she was getting the best of both options, helping those in dire circumstances and feeding her need for action and excitement.

As she thought about Josue and her reaction to him, she finished painting her mother's fingernails. 'There you go. Done for another week.'

Dorothy held her hands up to study her nails. 'Pretty colour. Thanks, darling. What about yours? You were wearing that purple shade last week.'

Sometimes there was nothing at all wrong with her mother's memory. 'I'll do mine tonight. Do you want to come shopping with me at Frankton? Megan's okay with it.' As long as she watched her like a hawk. 'We could get you a new jersey to go with those navy trousers you're wearing.' Replacing the pyjamas was the real reason for the trip, but she didn't want to raise the subject and possibly upset her mother's good mood.

'I haven't got any money at the moment. It's gone. I think someone stole it.'

Okay, not a perfectly clear mind after all. 'That's fine, Mum. I've got my wallet with me.' She covered all her mother's day-to-day expenses, while the unit she lived in here at the rest home was covered by the family trust her dad had set up when he'd learned he was ill.

'Then what are we waiting for? Shade, we're going out, my girl.'

CHAPTER FIVE

'THE ONE THING I don't miss from here is this damned cold.' Maisie was curled in on herself in the passenger seat, wearing one of Mallory's woollen coats and a knitted hat. She'd flown down late yesterday from Tauranga so she could visit Kayla today, and had stayed the night with Mallory. They'd sat up talking for hours, catching up on everything they'd been up to, including discussing the Frenchman living in Kayla's house, and getting Mallory to fess up about spending the night with him.

'So you've said at least ten times since stepping off the plane last night. You be careful on the road with my car when you drive it later.' Mallory grinned as she blew warm air on her clasped hands while waiting for the heater to warm up. With a thick puffer jacket over a wool jersey and thick shirt with a merino body-tight top under those, it was still freezing outside her warm house. The temperature gauge read minus nine degrees.

It had been a long, cold week, and not only due to the weather. Deliberately avoiding Josue had been hard. Longing woke her during the nights, and it had been impossible to make sense of the need and emotions and warnings swirling through her head. But she'd felt she had to do it, to at least appear nonchalant, and not dropping at his feet with longing.

'I'm not that out of practice,' Maisie muttered through her glove-covered hands. 'Not like you and men.'

'You want to walk to Wanaka, by any chance?'

'It'd be quicker than sitting here, trying to get warm.' Maisie laughed. 'You know I get homesick every time I visit. No one gives me a hard time like you.'

'Maybe you should think about returning. You can't let the Crim wreck your life forever.' Maisie's ex-husband was doing time for ripping off old ladies of their hard-earned savings.

Maisie was quiet for all of twenty seconds, then blurted, 'I have applied for a job at the hospital. It's in a new department being set up and won't start until next year.'

'My day just got better.' Mallory unclipped her seat belt and leaned over to hug her friend.

'About bloody time.' Yes, the three of them back in town at long last.

Maisie sniffed. 'Glad you agree.'

'You didn't think otherwise?'

'Not really.' The doubt was new for Maisie. But after all she'd been through because of the Crim it was no surprise.

'Cheer up. We'll have the rose petals all over the drive when you arrive. You can stay with me.'

'You might have a Frenchman living with you by then.'

'If you've got nothing better to say, then shut up.' Mallory put the car into gear and began backing out the drive. Her girlfriends got away with saying things no one else could, but Maisie's words hit home, racking up the doubts—should she remain out of contact while she still could?

A yawn ripped through her. The late night was catching up already. Except she'd been tired before she'd picked up Maisie yesterday.

Glancing up the road to Kayla's house, she noted Josue's car parked outside. His headlights had lit up her window as he'd driven home earlier after a night at work and she again thought of him lying in her bed, his body wrapped around hers. Shaking her head, she headed for the intersection, taking her time as black ice became apparent the nearer she got to the corner.

'Watch out,' she yelled as two cars sped past the end of her road in opposite directions. The back wheels of one began to slide. 'Don't brake,' she shouted, even though no one would hear her.

Brake lights glowed red and then an almighty bang reached her inside the car as the vehicles collided. The larger four-wheel drive stopped with its engine crushing the front and driver's side of the car. Two people in the front seats had been thrown forward into the broken mess.

'There's never a dull moment being a nurse.' Maisie was already undoing her seat belt.

Pulling over to one side, Mallory picked up her phone and tapped the most recent number she'd added to her contacts. Climbing out of her car, she felt relief when Josue answered immediately. 'Can you come down the road to the corner? There's been a serious head-on collision and I saw two people being tossed about inside one vehicle.'

'On my way.' And he was gone.

People were coming out of their houses all along the street. Two men were rushing to the accident, phones to their ears.

'I've rung a doctor,' she said when she reached them. 'And Maisie here's a nurse.'

'I'm onto 111 for fire and ambulance,' her neighbour told her.

'I'll hang up then,' the other guy said. 'Holy crap. This is a mess. Did you see what happened, Mallory?'

'The SUV lost it on the black ice.' She approached the squashed sedan and could see it hadn't been a front to front hit, but the side of the sedan was also caved in. Other people were gathering, some already trying to open the doors. Maisie pushed through. 'Excuse me, I'm a nurse.'

A familiar black vehicle braked to a halt beside them and Josue climbed out, a small leather bag swinging from his hand.

It was as though she'd been on a diet for days and now someone had handed her a plate of dessert. He was as stunning as she remembered, and as tall and broad as her body remembered, too. Gulp.

'Has anyone called an ambulance?' he called to her.

'Yes. And Maisie's here, over at the SUV. She's a nurse.' Mallory focused on the emergency as she made her way to the passenger side, where she could see a woman inside slumped against the console.

Josue was striding across to the mangled cars. 'Mallory, can you triage the passenger while I do the same with the driver?' he asked as he took in the details.

Pride filled her. He knew she was capable. 'Of course.' She smiled. Someone had brought a crowbar and was attempting to open the driver's door. At least the passenger door wasn't stuck. As she leaned in towards the woman, she called, 'Everyone, this is Josue Bisset. He's a doctor.'

Josue looked around. 'Anyone injured in the other vehicle?'

'Two tourists and they're are upright but complaining of pains in various places,' Maisie called.

'The fire truck's on the way,' someone else informed him.

Mallory squatted on her haunches, kneeling down to see what had happened to the passenger. 'Hello, I'm Mallory, a first-aid responder. Can you hear me? What's your name?'

'Pam. What happened?' Her eyes opened slowly, and she tried to look around but quickly shut them again.

'You've been in an accident. Can you move your legs?' From what she could see under the airbag it looked like Pam's left one was jammed solid.

The eyes opened again, pain reflecting out at Mallory. 'I can move the right a little, but it gets tight if I try to pull it up.'

'Best not to try any more. You might cause more swelling. I'm going to check your pulse and then look for any other injuries. Is that all right?'

Pam nodded. 'I think I banged my head on the side of the car. The seat belt dug into my chest hard.' Blood was oozing down the side of the woman's head.

'Josue, have you got sterile pads in your bag?' Mallory asked through the smashed windscreen. 'We've got a head wound here.'

'Yes. Help yourself. I'll take a look at the wound as soon as I can.' He hadn't looked up from examining his patient's face and was lifting her eyelids to check her eyes.

'I've got them,' a man called over the car. 'How many do you want, Mallory?'

'Two, thanks.' The wound reached from Pam's forehead to behind her ear. 'Any dizziness, Pam? Is your eyesight clear?'

'My eyes are a bit blurry. My head's throbbing.'

Her speech was strong and clear, despite the shock that must be setting in. The hit to her head can't have caused concussion then. 'You're doing well.' Fingers crossed. Mallory dabbed at the bleeding area on Pam's head with a pad before placing the second one over the whole wound. 'Right, let's see what your pulse is doing.' She reached for Pam's wrist.

'The fire truck's arrived,' someone announced from behind her. 'Ambulance is nearly here.'

Mallory continued counting the beats under her finger and timing a minute on her watch.

'Need you here, Mallory.' There was an urgency in Josue's voice that didn't bode well for the woman he was attending.

Mallory placed Pam's wrist on her thigh and leapt up, said to the closest person standing by, 'Hold her hand and talk to her, will you?' Then she dashed around to the other side of the car, where the door had been wrenched wide, exposing the injured woman. Mallory gulped at the carnage confronting her, but she didn't have time to stop and recover her breath. Josue had his fist pressed hard into the woman's inner thigh, blood everywhere. 'What can I do?'

'We need to get her out of here so I can put more pressure on this. The femur's fractured and torn the artery. Get those men to help you while I try and keep pressure on this.'

Looking across to the firemen, she called out, 'Jamie, over here fast. We have to retrieve this woman urgently, and Josue can't step away for a moment.'

Jamie instantly issued orders, at the same time

surveying the situation. 'Ryan, get a stretcher. Joe, with me. We'll take the shoulders and head. Nick, you take her legs. Josue, I'll tell you when to move and how. Mallory, you squeeze beside Josue and place your arms under her waist.'

She slipped into the minuscule space hard up against Josue and waited for Jamie to give the instructions.

'Take it slowly,' Josue warned. 'If I lose pressure, we have a problem.'

'Right. Ready. Everyone, slow lift now.'

Mallory's legs tightened and pinged with pain as she started to straighten, her arms taking the weight of the woman's torso as Josue struggled to stand up in the confined space while still pressing into that thigh.

'Keep lifting.' Jamie was watching everything like a hawk. 'Higher, Nick, counteract Josue pushing down. That's it. Right, everyone, one step away from the car. Another, another. That's it. She's free. Ryan, where's that stretcher?'

'Right here.'

'Okay, everyone, lower her onto the stretcher. One, two, three.'

Within moments the woman was lying on the stretcher and Mallory was on her knees beside her. 'Josue, want me to take over so you can do whatever else that's needed?'

'Yes. It won't be easy swapping places. We can't stop the pressure or she'll lose more blood. Clasp your hands into a fist like mine.' He nodded when she did so and said, 'Now put them hard against mine and push down at the same time as moving with me to replace my hands. Good. Keep going. Great. Stop. Now hold that pressure in place. Do not let up at all. Understand?'

'Yes.' She'd learned to do this in her advanced training, but actually doing it and having someone's life relying on her getting it right was frightening.

'You're great,' Josue said quietly.

Surely he meant *doing* great? It didn't matter. He made her feel special whatever he meant. 'So are you,' she replied equally softly. As a doctor, a lover and a man she already couldn't get enough of.

'Let's hope you're right.' He raised one eyebrow slowly and smiled. Then he straightened and looked around. 'Where's that ambulance?'

'Right here. Two more on the way,' Jamie informed them, reminding her she and Josue weren't alone here.

Of course, she knew they weren't but for a moment there she'd felt there was no one else around, even when her hands were pushed into a badly injured woman's thigh to hold back the bleeding that threatened her life. 'You going to hospital with this woman?'

Josue was shining a torch into the woman's eyes and getting no response. 'We need to fly her to Dunedin urgently.'

'Scott will be on standby at the airport.'

'Who calls him in?'

'You can. Or Jamie. My phone's in my pocket.' She held her breath at Josue touched her hip as he found the phone. 'There's a direct number under Emergency Rescue in Contacts.'

'Got it.' Josue punched the number and held her phone against his ear.

Mallory said, 'Tell Scott there's an empty section fifty metres from the intersection. The cops will keep everyone away for him to land.'

He nodded. 'Will do. Scott? This is Josue Bisset. We have an emergency out on the corner of Mallory's road.' He rattled off the street names with a quick glance her way. Checking he was right? Or remembering how he'd got the address wrong the other night? 'I have a woman needing to get to Dunedin Hospital fast—like yesterday. Good. Thanks.' He shoved the phone back in her pocket. 'He's lifting off now.'

Josue placed a hand on their patient's carotid artery, checking his watch. After a minute he lifted his fingers off the artery, a frown between his eyes. 'Low pulse here. And there was no response when I shone the torch directly into her eyes.'

'Head injury?'

'There's a soft area on the forehead I don't like.' His hands were spread over the scalp, his fingers careful as he searched for more damage.

Mallory glanced sideways through the car to Pam, who was now being attended to by the paramedic and first aider from the ambulance. 'Pam's pulse was normal five minutes ago,' she called across to them.

'Thanks, Mallory. Did the doc give her any painkillers in preparation for the engine being lifted away?'

'Not yet.' There hadn't been time, and she doubted if Josue carried restricted drugs with him. Checking she hadn't lightened the pressure on the wound beneath her hands, she looked over the thigh for any indications of other bleeding. Nothing, but there was a sharp shape to the trousers where the femur had broken. She shuddered at the thought of the pain that would've hit the woman at the moment of impact. In some ways it was best she was unconscious.

The heavy thumping of rotors filled the air, announcing Scott's arrival.

'At last,' Josue muttered as he wound a wide crepe bandage around his patient's head that a paramedic from a second ambulance had supplied at his request.

Mallory felt a similar relief, even though Scott had been fast getting here.

Within minutes the woman was being loaded into the chopper, Mallory still applying pressure until Josue could take over for the flight to Dunedin. With the other ambulances having now arrived, a paramedic was accompanying him. As Josue placed his hands over the still-bleeding site he said again, 'You're great.'

Straightening as far as the cramped interior allowed, she smiled and repeated her earlier reply. 'You too.' They were so in sync it warmed her throughout. He was a great doctor, and as for the man, great didn't begin to describe how she felt. If not for him, this woman's chances would be even slimmer. If not for him, her heart would be lying quietly, not beating a little harder and more erratically every time they interacted. 'We work well together.' Along with the other things that they did so well together. Her skin heated, and she had to resist the urge to reach out and take his hand. Wrong place, wrong time.

'Catch up tonight?' A hint of longing flitted through his eyes, quickly replaced with a nonchalance she didn't believe.

'I'd like that.' She'd restrained herself from calling in on him all week and suddenly she was more than ready to spend time with him again. 'I'll text you. I have to take Maisie to the airport.' Then she dropped out of the chopper onto the ground and rushed over to the wreckage without looking back, taking that smile and the warmth in his eyes with her.

'Mallory, I understand you witnessed the accident.' Zac was standing by the wreckage in his police uniform. 'I'll need to get some details when you've got a moment.'

'You can ask me too.' Maisie appeared from behind her. 'Hello, Zac.'

He must've cricked his neck at the speed he turned to stare at his best mate's sister. 'Maisie, how the hell are you?' And he stepped up to wrap her in his arms. 'Long time no see.'

Maisie grinned and leaned back to look up at him. 'If you didn't go bush so often, maybe you'd see me when I come to town.'

Mallory feigned a yawn. 'All right if we get on with this? Maisie and I are on our way to see Kayla in Wanaka.' If only these two would get over themselves and get together, she thought, but they were both stubborn as mules. 'This is what I saw happen, Zac.'

Josue parked outside Kayla's house and leaned back against the head rest. So much for a day off. First Mallory's call about the accident as he'd been about to drop into bed after a long night in the department, and then the flight to Dunedin, where their patient had immediately been admitted for urgent surgery. Despite the woman's heart stopping once due to blood loss and low blood pressure, she'd survived that far, and he was hopeful that once the surgeons had got her in Theatre her chances would rise. They'd promised to let him know later on today how she'd got on and what else they'd found.

He'd been dropped off at home by the paramedic after they'd returned to Queenstown. *Home?* Not the house necessarily, but he still felt comfortable in this town, with the people he worked with, and especially with Mallory. It was as though he belonged here, which he couldn't really. He didn't belong anywhere much except in Nice, and even there he tended to stay on the periphery of the group of friends he'd made through medical college and working in various hospitals.

As much as he'd hankered for caring friends and people to love him, as soon as he'd started getting close to anyone the old fears of being found lacking would start to haunt him.

Had he left some of his hang-ups behind when he'd come to this country? It was almost as though, because no one knew him, he could relax some of his fears of being rejected and therefore felt accepted.

Then there was Mallory. She added to, or was, the main reason he felt as though he'd found someone special that he could bond with. Like with Dean, he'd felt close to Mallory from the beginning. Unlike with Dean, there was a lot more in the closeness than just friendship. She was sexy and gorgeous and kept his veins bubbling just thinking about her.

Was she the reason Queenstown felt comfortable in a way nowhere else had for him? That couldn't be true. He had to be exaggerating the hunger for more to life than work and an occasional fling that had begun filling him from the night he'd met her. Hard to believe only one week ago she'd woken him on her couch, her eyes filled with questions and a warning not to be a smartass with her.

For two nights and two days he'd enjoyed her company over pizza and coffee, out in the bush, and getting very close in her bed. Then he hadn't set eyes on her until this morning. She was as beautiful as he'd remembered, as confident and capable dealing with the accident victims as she'd been with the boys last Saturday.

A sigh escaped. He'd missed her all week, especially when he hadn't been busy at work and had time on his hands. Twice he'd picked up his phone to call her. Both times he'd stared at her number, finger hovering above the screen as he'd thought hard. Should he call when he knew the day would come when he'd walk away? Already he knew he must not hurt her as he'd done Colette and Liza. She deserved better.

One evening he'd even debated walking down to her door and having a chat, sharing a coffee, catching up on what she'd been doing since they'd gone their separate ways after that amazing night in her bed. But she'd said no to seeing him last Sunday night, making him back off and give her some space. His heart had picked up when he'd suggested they get together tonight, and she hadn't hesitated to say yes. Relief had swamped him, quickly replaced with excitement. There was no stopping the sense that this time he might get it right.

As though there was more to come and he couldn't wait for it to unfold. Unbelievable. He hadn't done this in a long time, having decided it was best for everyone that he not get deeply involved. An occasional fling was one thing, safe and easy. This sense of knowing Mallory, of her knowing him, of wanting to find out more was new and exciting, but still scary.

A sharp wind rocked his vehicle, reminding him that his life at the moment included staying in this house while he worked at the local hospital, going on emergency medical flights to various cities and helping search for missing people. And perhaps even making friends, especially with a fascinating woman who lived only two hundred metres down the road.

There were a couple of hours to get through before Mallory turned up. It took only minutes to take off the filthy clothes he was wearing from working with the injured woman and throw them into the washing machine.

'Now what?' he wondered, looking around the immaculate living area. He could go for a drive along the lake and take a look around, but the idea didn't grip him. The day was getting on, cooling down rapidly, and he couldn't find any enthusiasm to go out. Was Mallory flying tourists around the mountains? He hadn't seen any sign of her at the airport when he'd got out of the rescue helicopter. But another woman had been with her at the accident so she could be anywhere. More likely she was probably on a tourist flight somewhere. What a fabulous job, flying around mountains and over lakes and taking people up to the snow-covered slopes.

Grr. He should be doing *something* instead of thinking about Mallory. Hadn't she mentioned mowing her lawn last weekend? It hadn't been done. Was that something he could do to ease this new restlessness winding through his veins?

He now had Kayla's number in his phone, so he texted her.

OK to use your mower to cut Mallory's lawn?

She came back in an instant. Help yourself. It's her mower anyway. You'll be her best friend forever. K

He laughed. Now, there was a good idea. Friends and then lovers? But they'd already made love. And he wanted to do that again, to hold Mallory and kiss her and run his hands over her satin skin. Friends next? Friendly lovers? Time to start on the lawn.

The mower in Kayla's shed was a ride-on and seemed to have as many gadgets as the helicopters Mallory flew. Typical of what he was getting to know about her. She certainly had a mechanical side to her brain. Plus a very feminine one, judging by the soft blouse and trousers she wore when not working, and the sexy lace panties and bra underneath that he'd had fun removing from her soft, warm body.

After a couple of minutes checking out the controls Josue got on board and started up, rode down the road and onto Mallory's lawn. He only hoped he'd got the settings right or there was going to be some explaining to do about chunks missing in the lawn. He hadn't used a ride-on before but it was a simple process once he figured out all the levers and buttons and soon he was driving around the massive lawn, quickly learning to dodge branches of trees strategically placed to take his head off if he wasn't vigilant.

The sun had almost disappeared behind the mountain when he finally rolled the mower into the shed and shut off the motor. The air was cold and crisp with the promise of another frost in the morning and yet Josue was warm with exhilaration. He'd enjoyed being outside in the crisp air and saving Mallory a chore this coming weekend. It also made him feel more at home than ever.

Careful, Jos. A mown lawn didn't make this his home or future. The warning didn't wipe the smile off his face or out of his chest, though. He fist-pumped as he headed inside for a sandwich. The fresh air had made him hungry.

The small stone-walled pub with a large open fire was busy as Mallory and Josue made their way up to the bar. 'Hey, Julie, how's things?' Mallory asked the girl pulling a beer.

'Great. I hear you went on the search for those boys last weekend. A good result.'

'It was.' She nodded to Josue. 'This is Josue Bisset. He was on the rescue too.' *By the way, he's wonderful.*

'Hi, Josue. Let me finish this order and I'll be right with you.'

Josue nodded, then looked at Mallory. 'You always know someone wherever you go.'

'That's what happens growing up in a small district, going to school and then working here. So many people are a part of that.'

'Have you done any travelling? Been overseas at all?'

'Once.' Not one of her favourite topics of discussion, her only trip abroad. She looked around. 'Shall I grab a table while there's one available?'

Josue's eyes narrowed a fraction, but all he said was, 'Sure. What do you want to drink?' So he'd noticed her reluctance to answer his questions.

Hopefully he wouldn't push it. 'A vodka and lime, thanks.'

She moved through the people crowded around tables and snagged one against the wall and hauled herself up onto a stool and rested her chin in her hand, trying to look dignified. The down side to being short was not being able to slip onto a bar stool with aplomb. She crossed her legs. The red leather ankle boots were her favourite winter accessory. They went with most of her outfits, and especially tonight's black fitted trousers and red-and-white shirt and black short jacket.

'Here you go.' Her vodka appeared in front of her.

She looked up into those intense eyes and smiled. 'Thanks.' Josue was so good looking she wanted to tighten her arms around herself and dance on the spot. He was with *her*, and he'd held her hand as they'd strolled through the town from his vehicle to here, making her feel special. Making her regret staying away over the week. It was time she'd never get back and she'd missed him. Strange, but it was how it was.

'I wouldn't have found this place without the GPS app on my phone.' He sat on the stool beside her. 'It's tucked away in such a narrow alley it's as though the owners don't want visitors finding it.'

'We know how good you are with your GPS.' She winked. 'Out-of-towners do find it, believe me. But it's a favourite with locals and we tend to crowd it out on certain nights of the week.'

'I'm glad you brought me here, though I probably won't be able to come back without you to lead the way.' He grinned and once again sent her blood heating. He did it too well.

How had she resisted calling him? Or going along the road to see him, sticking to her decision to take it slowly with him? Her restlessness over the need to find something more to her life had evolved into a need to spend more time with Josue and that had made her back off a little. 'I'll bring you again, promise.'

'*Merci*. I didn't even have to beg.' Josue laughed. 'Are you flying tomorrow?'

Anticipation began rising. 'I'm working tomorrow, but Sunday's mine. At this time of the year I usually do six out of seven days taking tourists on sightseeing flights or up to the ski fields with those who can afford it and prefer not to drive. What about you?'

'I have Sunday free too.'

'I want to go see Kayla again, take some things she asked for today. Would you like to come along and meet her? I could show you around the area afterwards.' It was the first she'd known she was going to make that suggestion. *A damned good one, Mallory.* It was time she got over holding out on having some fun with Josue. One week had been wasted already, and if he turned out to be as wonderful as she already hated to admit she thought he was, then she didn't want to lose any more time. She should get on and make the most of his time in Queenstown and deal with the consequences when they happened because she could no longer pretend she wasn't interested.

Josue leaned over and brushed her cheek with his lips. 'Count me in.'

His aftershave was spicy and light and set her aglow inside. Sipping her cool drink did nothing to chill the heat. Neither did the sudden need to open up to him some more. Wasn't getting to know him meant to include sharing herself and to take some steps towards risking allowing him to know more than she usually put out there?

'About me and travel, I've only been to Australia and then only to the outback. I did spend a few days in Brisbane on the way over, which was exciting, but most of my time was spent north of there on stations or farms.'

Surprise had slipped into Josue's gaze. Not expecting her to return to his earlier question? 'What did you do over there?'

'Crop dusting with a helicopter, and I took cattle owners out over their stations to find stock. The stations are huge, endless really, and flying is the easiest way around when they're not herding cattle, though they sometimes use choppers for that too. The dust can be horrendous and the heat is way beyond anything I'd ever experienced. The flies drove me crazy too.' It'd been an interesting six months, but she wouldn't be repeating it, and that had nothing to do with Hogan even when he'd been the reason she'd come home.

Josue was shaking his head and laughing. 'Anyone else I've asked about their overseas trips has talked about cities and historic buildings or sights like canyons or mountains, not flying in dust and dealing with flies. Mallory, you are something else.' He leaned in for another kiss, this time on the corner of her mouth.

She laughed with him. 'Maybe one day I'll get to travel to your part of the world and be the tourist with a camera around my neck as I take in all the sights I've heard so much about from the tourists I fly around here.'

'Let me know if you want to do that and I'll be your guide.' He stared her, then took a large gulp of his beer. 'I guess you won't be leaving Queenstown in a hurry with your mother here.'

Laying her hand on his thigh, she squeezed lightly. *Too intimate, Mallory?* Or was she getting on with letting go the restlessness? 'You're right. I'm not going anywhere as long as Mum's around. And to be fair, I've not thought a lot about travelling. It's never been something I've wanted to do.'

'So what made you go to Australia?' The steady look coming her way said he knew there was more than a straight-out job offer from a company that did helicopter work, and he'd have picked up on her abrupt answer the first time he'd mentioned her travelling.

Her glass was cool in her warm hand as she turned it in a circle on the table. Hadn't she wanted to let Josue in a little? In that case, she should tell him about Hogan. *All of it?* In order to trust Josue, she would see how it felt to tell him what she'd told no one else except Kayla and Maisie about Hogan's betrayal. 'I followed my boyfriend.'

Josue tipped his head to the side a little. 'This sounds interesting.'

Her smile surprised herself. 'Actually, it was.' As well as infuriating. 'I met Hogan when he worked a summer here on the river jet boats. We got on brilliantly so when he asked if I'd go to Australia with him when he went home, I was thrilled. I got a job and everything was wonderful.' So far so good. She sipped her drink.

Josue was watching her quietly. His hand covered hers for a brief moment. 'It was easy to get work?'

'Hogan's family helped by putting out the word in their district and soon I was busier than I'd ever been. It's an amazing place, being beyond the cities and towns, where everyone has to be strong and rely on each other to get through all that nature throws at them. I did like it, but it would never be somewhere I'd want to live forever.'

'Not even for love?'

'We never got far enough in our relationship for me to have to decide. Yes, I loved Hogan, but he'd often said he wanted to move to the coast and work in the tourist industry. He applied for plenty of positions but he couldn't get one he liked. He didn't want to start at the bottom. That's when his frustration started growing and I became the target for criticism. I didn't cook his favourite meal properly, made the bed wrong, was always at work when he wanted me. I started falling out of love and decided to come home.'

'I'm guessing you've been here ever since.'

She nodded. 'Yes, and no regrets.'

'There's more, isn't there?'

Mallory gasped. 'You're too clever for your own good.' Why not tell him? Usually she locked down on what Hogan had done because it made her feel and look stupid. But really it was no big deal and if she told someone, like Josue, then she might finally forgive Hogan. 'Hogan didn't take my leaving very well. He was furious. When I returned to our flat to pack up I discovered he'd emptied my bank accounts of every last cent.'

'He had your details?'

'We were in a relationship. I trusted him, otherwise why was I there?' Her mouth flattened. 'I won't do that again, I was stupid.' She'd given her trust and expected it to be reciprocated. It had been a painful lesson, and one hard to forget. She doubted she'd be quite so trusting so readily again about anything close to her heart.

Her hand was suddenly in Josue's, his fingers between hers. 'Not at all. You did what you believed was right.'

'That's fine until it went belly up. I didn't see it coming and I should've. He was always complaining about not having enough money for projects and yet spent all his earnings very freely.' She smiled at Josue, feeling happy about having told him. He seemed to understand why she felt so bad about herself, except now she didn't any more. She had made a mistake but it was in the past and she'd recouped her savings by working long hours and had had fun while doing it.

Josue leaned in and placed a kiss on her lips. 'Why am I the first you've told?'

Another gasp. 'How do you do that? Read me like a pamphlet advertising a trip on Lake Wakatipu?' It should be frightening, but it wasn't. She accepted his ability to understand her. Did that mean she was accepting him as more than a man to have a fling with? And why wasn't *that* scaring the daylights out of her if it was true? He had already warned her he'd move on regardless.

'I honestly don't know,' Josue admitted, looking a little confused. 'But I feel I know you. Strange when we haven't known each other long, but it's been like that from the beginning.'

He was admitting that? Did he understand how that was pulling her further into him? Mallory shook her head. There were no straightforward answers and she was tired of thinking too much about Josue leaving. She just wanted to get on and enjoy his company. Get closer and share their free time doing the things they both liked.

'Want another beer?' Then food, a walk around the town, and home to bed. It sounded like a good plan to her, one that warmed her throughout, including her heart. *Careful, Mallory.*

He said, 'Think I'll have a wine and order a steak, then take you for a stroll down to the wharf. After that we'll go home for some rest and recreation.'

Mallory was still laughing at his mind-reading skills when he returned with another round of drinks.

CHAPTER SIX

THREE WEEKS OF shared meals and bed, of laughter and in-depth conversations about everything except where they were going with this fling, and Josue was still smitten. More so. It seemed he couldn't get enough of Mallory.

Now at the top of the ski slope, Mallory looked gorgeous dressed in bright red skiing clothes and matching helmet and gloves. She was grinning like the cat with the cream as she studied the slope in front of her.

Until he tapped his glove-covered fist against hers and said, 'Last one to the bottom buys dinner.' Then he was gone, not waiting for her to agree or even turn to face in the downward direction. She could easily outrun him given half a chance, which he wasn't doing.

'Cheeky bugger,' she called.

'*Oui*, that's me.' He hadn't had such an enjoyable day in a long time. Seemed whatever they did together was fun and made them closer still.

The skis skidded under him as he spun around and lunged his poles into the snow to push for more speed. 'I'm not buying dinner tonight.' But he was talking to air, or the other skiers standing around who he had to zigzag through to avoid crashing into someone. A quick glance behind showed Mallory having the same difficulty and had slowed up to dodge an accident. *Good.*

He aimed for the side of the slope where it was less congested, concentrating on keeping his skis parallel and his hips moving in unison with them as he swerved left then right down the steep slope. They were on the top field, where only experienced skiers went, and with fewer people up here and no young children learning to ski it gave a freedom he relished. Up here he could forget everything but the cold air rushing past his face and the glitter of the last of the sun on the snow. It was magic, made even more so today because Mallory was with him. Not right now, though. He was still ahead but not by much.

The urge to let rip and speed straight down, to whizz away, gripped him. Only the thought of losing control on the sharper slope coming up made him hold back and continue as he was.

Whish, whish. That wonderful sound of the snow under skis came from the left. Mallory was closing the gap. He squinted ahead. There was some way to go to the bottom. No way dinner was going to be on him.

Whish, whish. He pushed harder to the other side where the snow was less churned up. He didn't see the small rock until almost on it. Jerking sideways, his balance went from under him and, splat, he hit the snow hard. His skis snapped off his boots, his body sprawled wide.

'Josue?' Mallory swept up to him. 'Are you all right?' Her eyes were full of worry.

Shoving upwards, he stood, clipped his boots onto the skis. 'I'm fine.'

'Are you sure?'

'Two broken legs and a twisted arm.' He grinned as he reached for his poles. 'You going to help me?'

She pulled a face at him. 'You might as well order the pizzas now.' She was off, aiming for the markers for the end of the run now less than two hundred metres away.

'Make mine a Hawaiian with extra pineapple, will you?' Josue swept past her right before the line.

'That sweet tooth won't do you any favours,' she muttered through gasps of air.

'Bad loser?' He stood before her, dragging in air through his smile at a similar rate to her.

Good. It hadn't been a doddle for him either. Not after he'd taken that fall.

'Not a bad run for an old bloke,' she quipped.

'An *injured* old bloke.' He laughed.

She suddenly went serious on him. 'You didn't hurt yourself, did you?'

Wrapping an arm over her shoulders, he pulled her close and kissed her cheek. 'Doubt I'll even have a bruise to show for it.' She wouldn't be able to kiss him better. Damn.

'Let's head on down and go home. I'm thinking a bowl of hot soup and steaming bread rolls sound especially good now. Better than pizza.'

The air was cooling rapidly now that the sun was dropping behind the mountain. All around them skiers were making their way down the lower slope to the main buildings and the car parks. 'It's been great having a day to ourselves, no calls from S and R.'

'No emergencies where I was needed at the hospital. *Oui,* a perfect day.' Josue hugged her again. 'And it's not over yet.' He did love being with Mallory. *Whoa.* His arm dropped to his side. *Getting too involved, Jos.*

Then Mallory was leaning into him, those bright eyes twinkling mischievously. 'You want another race down the next slope?'

He couldn't stop the laughter bubbling up and out. Reaching for her, he wound his arms around her lithe body and kissed her long and hard, drinking in all that was Mallory. To hell with everything else. Right now, out here in the fresh, crisp air on the side of a stunning mountain he was happy beyond belief.

Mallory looked up at him, a twinkle in her eyes. 'I like it when you smile like you don't have a care in the world.'

'So do I.' And he truly did.

A shout came from behind them.

Reluctantly Josue broke their eye contact and looked around. He held his breath as he watched a skier speed down the slope too fast, his body hunched in a racing pose, poles sticking out behind him.

'Why do I think this is going to end badly?' Mallory muttered.

Suddenly the skier twisted abruptly and tumbled, rolling over and over, the skis flicking off one at a time as cries were heard. Then the skier slammed deep into the snow on his back.

Josue headed for the person, Mallory right beside him. 'So much for a day off, huh?' He dropped to his knees beside the skier. 'Hello, I'm Josue. Can you hear me?'

'Yes,' a male voice answered. 'What happened?'

'You lost control on your run and fell. I'm a doctor. What's your name?'

'Ian. My leg hurts.'

Mallory was opposite and already checking for signs of injury. 'Josue.' She pointed to the man's thigh. A broken ski pole was sticking into the muscle.

'This where it hurts?' Josue asked Ian as he gently pressed around the pole entry. The pole had gone in quite a way. Best to leave it there until the guy was in the sterile environment of a hospital. Pulling the pole out could also cause more serious bleeding.

'Yes.' The guy was pushing himself up on his elbows.

'Careful. You might have other injuries.' He might have done damage to his spine with all that rolling.

'I'm good.' Ian looked at his bloodied leg and gulped. 'Oh.' He flipped backwards.

'He's fainted,' Mallory said as she continued feeling both legs for more injuries.

People were gathering around. Then a woman stepped up. 'I'm Jane, an instructor here. Do I need to get medical help?'

'I'm a doctor. Mallory here has first-aid skills. We're going to need assistance moving this man down to the main building, where he'll need to be transported to hospital.'

'Someone got lucky, crashing right in front of

you two,' said the instructor. 'I'll be back with
the mobile sled.'

'I guess he was.' Josue smiled at Mallory before looking for evidence of any other injuries.
He found nothing, then ran his fingers over Ian's
skull. No signs of injury there either. 'Hey, Ian,'
he called. 'Wake up.'

'What happened?' Ian croaked.

'You fainted. Now, tell me, are you hurting
anywhere else? Your head?' There could be a
concussion or an internal bleed from the trauma
of slamming into the snow.

'A bit wobbly, that's all.' This time he sat up
slowly, looking everywhere but at his thigh.
Lifting the opposite leg off the snow, he gri-
maced. 'Something not right with my left ankle.'

Mallory began undoing the laces of Ian's
boot. 'I'm not taking the boot off, just trying to
relieve the pressure. You've got some swelling
going on. Whether it's broken or just sprained
won't be apparent until you've had an X-ray.'

'Whichever, I won't be skiing any time soon,
will I?' Ian grunted. 'My own fault, I suppose,
but that run was too good not to race down.'

'You're not wrong there, mate.'

Another man had slid to stop a couple of metres away. 'Is Ian all right?' he asked. 'We're together,' he added quickly.

Josue was saved from answering when a four-wheeled, covered bike with a sled hitched to the back arrived and Jane leapt off. 'I've got a stretcher we can load the man onto and then lift him onto the tray,' she said to Josue. 'One of you want to ride with him? There's room in front for one of you and your gear.'

He'd forgotten about his skis and poles. 'Thanks. I'll go on the sled, keep Ian from moving too much. Let's get him loaded and down to the warmth of indoors.'

'I've notified the on-site medical crew at headquarters and they're arranging for the ambulance to be ready when we get down.' Jane was laying the stretcher beside Ian.

'I don't need that,' he grumbled and tried to stand up on one leg, and sat down abruptly with a groan.

'Let's do it our way.' Josue put a hand on the man's arm. 'Shuffle your butt across.' He looked Mallory's way. 'I'll see you down the bottom?' At her nod, he moved to sit on the bike.

Ten minutes later Jane pulled up beside the waiting ambulance, Mallory and Ian's friend joining them moments later. 'Just in time to help us get your mate aboard,' Josue told him.

With Ian inside the vehicle, Josue and Mallory gave a short account to the paramedic of the extent of the injuries they'd noted and headed towards the car park. Josue reached for Mallory's free hand. 'It was still a great day.'

'I never count helping someone as bad. Even when it disrupts a perfect day.' She grinned and leaned in to kiss him.

The alarm went off at five thirty. Monday morning once more. Another week about to kick off. Mallory groaned as she rolled over and tapped off the irritating buzzing, then yawned hard. She'd been doing a lot of that lately, but then there'd been plenty of nights in bed with Josue and evenings out for S and R meetings and meals at the pub. Her life had gone from busy to busier and she was loving it.

A large hand was splayed over her hip, kneading softly. Her legs were entangled with Josue's. Another amazing night. She'd thought it couldn't get any better after the first time they'd gone to bed yet every time was better than before. 'Why can't it be snowing and howling a gale?'

'You don't want to go to work?' came a low growly question from her shoulder, where Josue had tucked in his chin.

'Can't say the idea's enthralling me even when I'm only doing half a day. I've got my medical this afternoon.' The regular check required by the pilots' licensing board seemed to have come round fast. Hard to believe a year had gone by since the last one.

She tossed the cover aside and sat up, legs over the side. If she didn't move now she might never get up. Not that she had a lot of energy left for getting up close with Josue, but this was more than her body aching from yesterday's skiing on Coronet Peak with this wonderful man. It was odd because she didn't usually feel too bad after a day on skis. Might ask her GP, who did the pilot medicals, if there was anything doing the rounds she might've caught from one of the many people she came into contact with through her job.

'Hey, that's cold.' Josue grabbed back the cover.

'Sure is.' Goose bumps were rising on her skin now that she wasn't curled up against Josue. 'I'm having a shower.' But first she'd put the kettle on.

In the kitchen she paused at the sight on the floor by the bench. The last of the pizzas from last night had disappeared except for some crumbs. 'Shade, naughty girl.' It was her own fault for not tidying up before going to bed with Josue.

Shade lifted her head from her bed and wagged her tail.

'Come on. Outside while I get ready for work.'

No point making a fuss about the mess now. Shade would've forgotten what she'd done, or that she'd been naughty. It had been a golden opportunity and she'd taken it. Mallory laughed. Couldn't really blame her girl for that. She'd have done the same.

Holding the back door open, she stared at Shade until she grudgingly got up and walked out. It might be the morning ritual but in winter Shade never leapt off her bed with any exuberance.

In the shower, standing under hot water, arms crossed over her tender breasts, Mallory tipped her head back to wash the sleep away. 'Damn, forgot to put the kettle on.'

The bathroom door opened and Josue strolled in, definitely the man of her dreams in all his naked glory. What a body, with not a gram of fat—he was all muscle. Elbowing the door wide, she moved to one side to make room for him.

He was eyeing her with tenderness.

Her throat clogged. That tenderness for her was…was special and growing on her. She felt as though she was melting into a puddle at her feet. Her eyes were wet, not only from the shower but from the emotions he created within her. This was what she'd been looking for. She looked up at him, her insides all mushy with love. *Really?* Yes, really. It was fast, but everything felt right about this man, different from her previous experiences. He just fitted with her focus on work and caring for people and how he relaxed at home and shared the chores. The list was endless. Regardless of his warning about not staying around, she hadn't been able to avoid falling for him.

'Josue,' she whispered, and reached up to run her fingers over his chest.

He stood still, looking into her as though he was reading her heart. Though his eyes were light, not grave as they usually were when he spoke about leaving, so she hoped he had no idea what was going in on her head.

Her lungs were still, her heart beating in erratic little patters like it was trying to kickstart her breathing. Yes, this was love. Though where could it lead? She had no idea and was afraid to ask in case he ran from the shower and she never saw him again. She'd always known this could happen and she'd chosen to accept the consequences, whatever they were, right from the outset.

'Mallory.' Josue placed his hands on her arms, his gaze still caught in hers, and he leaned in to place a kiss on her chin. 'Turn around.'

She stared at him for a moment. He meant everything to her. It had happened fast. *Now what?* They would carry on regardless, making the most of the time they had together. She turned around.

Josue began soaping her skin with gentle strokes, starting at her shoulders, easing the kinks out of her muscles, and slowly working lower down her back and over her backside.

She began relaxing under his touch. Was this Josue saying how much he cared for her? Showing, not telling her? Had he seen her love in her eyes? Or was he avoiding her truth? Not wanting her to love him?

His hands were on her waist, bringing her around to face him so he could start again on her breasts. His eyes were still light and his mouth soft. Then he stopped and leaned into kiss her.

She was so confused. What did Josue want? Glancing down, she saw he was ready for her, but when she reached for him, he smiled and shook his head. 'We haven't got time.'

Now there was a challenge if ever she'd heard one. Her hand wrapped around him. 'You think?' Josue was ready for her, wanted her, and despite her confusion she was going to show him how much she cared for him.

Josue laughed as he drove into the hospital car park. 'Never say that to Mallory unless you've got spare time, Jos,' he said to himself. Not that they'd needed long, they knew how to bring each other to a climax in an instant. Now he felt on top of the world when he was literally at the bottom of the globe, talking to himself out loud. But how was a man supposed to act when he'd just had another amazing night with a woman who turned him on with a look and followed through with so much more it was almost unbelievable? Almost but not entirely, because time and again he'd experienced Mallory's lovemaking and knew it was for real. And the feelings he had for Mallory were growing all the time. Truly. They were. It felt like love. Not that he had experienced it like this before, but if he was to fall in love this was how he wanted it to be. It felt real. Was he ready? How did he know?

There'd been a moment in the shower when Mallory had gone quiet on him, her eyes darkening as though she'd had something big to say. When she hadn't, he'd felt relieved and disappointed all at once. To hear what might fall from those lips could change his world forever. What if Mallory had come to care for him? Even love him? His heart began racing. Did she? It would be beyond his wildest dreams.

Then she'd smiled, her eyes lightening as she'd laid a hand on his chest. A loving gesture that had softened him. He'd begun soaping her body and they'd made love and he'd been happy. He was fitting in so well with Mallory, with his work and the search and rescue mob that he might really be finding his place. He wanted that, and he was beginning to think this time he just might be able to give as good as he got—with Mallory.

There was so much more than the lovemaking that was special with her. Lying spooned together, his arm around her waist, hearing her gentle breaths as she slept, sharing a hastily put-together meal, yesterday on the ski field, challenging each other. It gave him a sense of homecoming, of having found what he'd been looking for all his life, and that had struck him so deeply he might not be able to let go again.

Mallory was at the centre of everything happening to him. Should he be protecting himself or letting go and diving in? He'd spent his life looking for love and not finding it, Gabriel and Brigitte being the exceptions. Theirs was the sort of love a child required, bringing with it guidance and support and kindness. Until now he'd believed he was too unreliable, wouldn't be able to give stability to any relationship. And now? There was the thing. He had no idea. Except now he wanted to try, wanted to let these loving feelings take over to the point he was starting to think he could do it, could be there for Mallory through all the hurdles that life would throw at them.

The air was cold outside his car. Josue hunched his shoulders and headed inside to the department, his phone pressed to his ear, wanting to hear her voice.

'You've reached Mallory Baine. Please leave me a message and I'll get back to you.' Josue pressed off and then phoned again to listen to her voice, his gut turning into a tight ball as he left his message, 'Hey, it's me. Have a great day. See you later.'

'Josue, you're early,' the department head called from the centre desk as he made his way along the row of empty beds. 'Didn't you sleep last night?'

'No.' Not a lot of sleeping going on where he'd been. 'I woke up early so figured I might as well make myself useful.'

'Your timing's perfect.' John stood up. 'Feel like a coffee?'

'You have to ask?' What did John want to talk about at this hour?

John headed for his office where there was always coffee to be had. 'We've been quiet all night so I've had time to catch up on some paperwork.' He filled two mugs and passed one to Josue before closing the door. 'Grab a seat.'

This was shaping up to be a serious conversation. 'What's up?'

'This is confidential, all right?'

'Yes.'

'Jason's had a cancer diagnosis.'

The older doctor had been looking a bit jaded over the past month. 'I am sorry to hear that. I've heard so much about his cycling exploits it doesn't seem possible.'

'It's been a shock for those in the know. Jason's decided to step back from work—to resign, in fact. It's a serious diagnosis and he'd prefer to spend the time with family and doing a couple of things he's not got around to before.' John sipped his coffee thoughtfully. 'So I'm offering you a permanent position. I know you intend on returning to France next month but you've mentioned that your visa runs for another year. If you accepted the offer and wanted to stay on longer than the twelve months we'd be your sponsor for a resident's visa.'

Josue's chest tightened. Him take on a permanent position? He enjoyed working in this small hospital and had integrated with everyone easily. The work was stimulating so what more could he want? If he said yes it would be for at least a year, and possibly more. Excitement began fizzing in his veins. Then stopped. This would mean settling down, staying put in a town where Mallory lived, even if he got cold feet and called off their relationship. That's how he'd stayed safe in the past. Being able to leave. What if he were to take a chance and let Mallory fully into his life? If she was about to tell him she loved him then this was perfect. She was all he needed, wanted. *What? All I want? As in she really might be the one?* Yes, wasn't that what he'd been trying to tell himself? He loved her. He stared around, looking for a distraction from this blindside, and came up against John's steady gaze as he waited for an answer. He had a job offer that went some way to making this easier. Though it was as if the decisions were being taken out of his hands. A job offer and Mallory seeming to have something important to tell him. He still had to return home for Gabriel's operation, but he could return afterwards, and make a go of it with Mallory. Sharp pain squeezed his chest. If he'd read her correctly, and so far he'd always got it right with her.

'Josue?' John finally asked. 'Are you all right?'

Not at all. Why did the idea of Mallory being the love of his life feel more right than anything he'd ever known? This was too much. He couldn't concentrate, couldn't make any decisions right now. 'I'm surprised.' Surprised didn't begin to describe his emotions. He was overwhelmed, grateful, happy, *terrified*. Not of the job but of finally falling in love. Darling Mallory. He had to get out of here. 'Thank you for the offer.' *Be sensible. Don't rush it.* 'But I do have to be back in Nice next month.'

'Are you at all interested in a permanent position?'

'There's a lot to consider.' He'd love to stay if he could get past the constant fear of rejection when it came to settling down. *Give it a go.* Did he have it in him? He might lose his heart. But anything worth holding onto took effort and determination. Or so he'd been told.

'How about you take the rest of the week to think about it? After that I'll have to start looking further afield, but I'd like you to come on board. You've fitted in well with everyone and our systems.'

Josue nodded agreement. 'Sounds fair. I am keen, but there're things I have to look into.' *Give it a go. Stop overthinking.* He drained his coffee. Fresh air would be great even if it was freezing cold, but walking around the streets wasn't going to bring any answers. Only talking to Mallory could do that and he wasn't quite ready to lay his heart on the line and tell her about this offer. It was his decision to make. And he needed to absorb the knowledge he was falling for her too. Two hits in one go.

The caution he held close had kept him out of trouble before and it could save him from making a complete fool of himself this time. Was he really falling for her? If so, then, yes, he wanted the job. If not, he had to get away fast so as not to hurt her. And himself. *Too late for that one.*

John's phone rang.

Josue stood up. 'I'll get out of your way.'

'Sure.'

Josue's phone beeped as he stepped into the corridor and it took all his control not to rip it from his pocket. It had to be Mallory. No one else would be texting him. Unless it was S and R but they knew he was working today. He reached for the phone and smiled as happiness filled him. Happiness or love? *Both.*

S and R training tonight. Eat out first?

How could he have forgotten the training meeting? Oui. Pick you up at 6.00.

Damn. He'd needed time to work through everything that had happened but he'd answered without thinking. *See?* A knot formed in his gut. Staring at the phone, his heart squeezed. If he admitted to loving her it couldn't be a dabble in the water, he'd have to dive right in. He still had to go to France and help Gabriel. He owed that man so much. But once home would he be able to come back to Mallory, or would he stay away, letting the old fears of failure and rejection win? The knot tightened painfully. He swore.

'Josue, we've had a call.' A nurse appeared from a cubicle. 'The ambulance is on its way with a woman kicked in the stomach by her horse.'

Time to get on with why he'd come to Queenstown in the first place. He put his phone and Mallory back in his pocket where he could reach either of them in an instant. If only he could shove these sudden doubts away as easily. 'I'm coming.'

'Everything is in perfect working order.' Sara folded the blood-pressure cuff. 'I wish all my patients were like you.'

'Then you wouldn't have any,' Mallory retorted around a smile that quickly faltered. 'I'm glad I've passed. But there's one thing.' She hesitated. This was silly. What was a bit of exhaustion here and there? Except it had become so constant over the last few days she was starting to worry something serious was happening.

'Go on.' Sara was typing in her notes.

'I'm so tired all the time. It's getting worse. I have to drag myself out of bed every morning. I went skiing yesterday but most of the time I wasn't exactly speeding.' Except for the last run, trying to outrun Josue.

'Any other symptoms?'

'Like what?'

'Pain, aches, nausea, headaches.'

'None of the above.'

'You're eating all right?'

'Yes.' Ah, no. 'I didn't have breakfast this morning, and last night only two pieces of pizza. But that's no big deal.' She stared at the doctor. 'Come to think of it, I felt queasy on the drive to the mountain yesterday.'

'When was your last period?'

Her eyebrows lifted as she stared at Sara. What was Sara saying? No. She couldn't be. Nausea rose fast. 'Where's the bathroom?'

'Take deep breaths. It's through that door if you need it.' Sara sat back in her chair, waiting as Mallory sucked in lungfuls of air then huffed them out.

Her hands were tight balls on her thighs, her head spinning. This had to be a mistake. Deep breath. When did Josue arrive? He'd been here over a month. It was possible, but they'd taken precautions. A memory of the first time rose in her mind. 'July. Early July was my last one.' As the words spewed out her body slumped in the chair. This was not happening.

'Then we'd better find out if you're pregnant, don't you think?' Sara asked.

Mallory could only nod as despair took over. She couldn't have a baby on her own. It wasn't right. What would Josue say? If he wasn't interested in staying around for a relationship then he'd hardly want a baby to hold him down.

'Mallory, first things first. Let's do the urine test and find out if it's positive.'

She was. The blue line mesmerised her. A baby. *Her* baby. 'Is this real?' She'd dreamed of this day, and had feared it wouldn't happen. But she wasn't in a relationship. Josue was leaving.

'Yes, it is. I'm going to take a blood sample for an HCG to find out how far along you are.' Sara looked over at her. 'One step at a time, okay?'

'I had an ectopic pregnancy when I was eighteen.' Josue was leaving.

'That doesn't mean you won't go full term with this one if that's what you want. It's rare for a woman to have two ectopic pregnancies and you haven't mentioned any symptoms that suggest this is anything but normal. You'd have known something was wrong well before now if your dates are right. However, I'll arrange a scan for you at the earliest possible time. It'll mean going to Invercargill.'

Mallory's head was spinning with the speed

at which this was happening. She'd come for a pilot medical and was now pregnant and going for a scan. What had just happened to her day? Her life? Within minutes everything had changed radically. 'I'll go. I'm only going to worry myself sick until I know for certain this is a normal pregnancy.' Mallory gasped. Pregnant? Her? 'Am I really having a baby?'

Sara nodded. 'You are. Is that good news?'

'Yes.' The answer was out without any thought. It was true. It might be unexpected, and she had no idea what lay ahead with Josue, but, yes, it was the best news. She was already accepting it. But of course she would. This was what she'd wanted in her future—but her dream had included a man to love too. Not a man who said he wasn't staying around, who didn't believe he was capable of settling in one place and being happy. If that meant she'd have to raise a child on her own then she would. There was already a warm protectiveness for her child growing inside her. Her life had changed in the last few minutes.

Josue. Her heart squeezed with love. How was she going to break the news to him? He cared for her, she knew he did whether he admitted it or not. Yet having a baby was a game changer. Josue would probably take the next plane out of the country, leaving her as Jasper had done with her first pregnancy. Despite his upbringing in foster care she didn't trust him not to make sure his own child never went through that anguish. He might want to, but staying around to be there all the time was a big ask for him. She sank further down the chair. She had to find a way to convince him to stay, to work at being a dad, to accept her love. Could she trust him when Jasper had run in this same situation? What if it *was* an ectopic pregnancy? Would he be relieved, just like Jasper had been, released from his responsibilities?

'Mallory, slow down. I can see the questions spinning through your mind. Take it easy. It's only been minutes since you found out. Let me take the blood, and then I suggest you go for a walk, get some air and just absorb the fact you're pregnant. One step at a time.'

'Sure.' That easily?

It was freezing cold outside and Mallory's nose felt numb within minutes of stomping along the path. A baby. Her hand lay over her belly. *Hello. Who are you? Are you comfortable in there?* At least it'd be warmer in there than out here.

How *was* she going to tell Josue? It would be a huge shock. She'd just been hit with the news and was slowly coming to grips with it. This wasn't something that could be put on hold until she felt ready to deal with it. Josue avoided issues by leaving, it was his go-to reaction. The real question was how to make him pause and consider everything. Her teeth were grinding, making them ache horribly. She didn't have a damned clue how to deal with any of this. Why spend time wondering about what Josue would do? Because she needed him at her side. More than that, she needed him to love her—for herself, not only as the mother of his child.

She stamped her boot on the hard ground and broke the ice covering the grit. *I'm pregnant.*

Unplanned, unexpected and a whole new beginning. Would this really shut down her restlessness now there was something—*someone*—to plan for? Yes, a baby was a wonder. One she'd begun to think she'd never experience when she hadn't found a man to love and be with forever. She'd finally met Josue, and loved him. As for the rest of that picture, that was nothing but a blank at the moment. She had to talk to him. First, she'd need to get used to the fact she was having a baby.

A gust of icy wind slapped her, sending shivers through her. What if the pregnancy *was* ectopic? She hadn't experienced any stomach pains like the first time so it couldn't be. *Don't get ahead of yourself or you might tempt fate.*

Enough. She headed for her car. She'd go and see Kayla, picking up Shade from home on the way.

Checking her phone, she saw three texts from Kayla. Apparently she was going stir crazy with boredom.

I'm on my way, she texted, and headed towards Wanaka, where she might tell Kayla her news and have a good old talk about everything.

That didn't happen. Kayla wanted to get out of the house, said her parents were driving her crazy by not letting her do a damned thing during her recovery. Her concussion was long gone, but the left leg ached all the time and the other with a compound fracture gave constant stabs of pain giving cause for her parents insisting on her staying put on the couch. 'I've done nothing but rest for weeks and I'm going to become less active than a statue if I don't do something. Get me out of here.'

After cramming Kayla and her crutches onto the back seat of the car with her legs up and a seatbelt twisted across her body, and leaving Shade at the house, Mallory drove into town and a bar where they eventually sat drinking juice while Kayla vented and Mallory tried to listen and not think about Josue and the baby. When her song started playing, she stared at the name showing on her phone. What did she say? *Hi, having a great day? Wish you were here?* Reluctantly she picked it up. 'Hello, Josue.'

'Mallory, thank goodness. Where are you? I'm waiting to pick you up but there's no sign of you at home.'

She swore. The S and R meeting. Josue had said they'd go for something to eat first. 'I'm sorry. I'm with Kayla. I forgot all about the meeting.'

'You forgot? What's wrong?'

Everything. 'Nothing. Kayla was having a bad day and I came over to cheer her up. That's all.'

'Really?' Silence hung between them. He obviously wasn't satisfied with her answer.

She'd let him down. 'Really. I won't be going to the meeting now. I'll let them know.'

'You sure there's nothing wrong?'

She was hardly going to tell him over the phone. 'Josue, I am sorry.' Yet she'd forgotten they were going for a meal. Not surprising, but he didn't know why. 'I'll make it up to you, I promise.' *With the news that you're going to be a father.* She swallowed hard.

'I'll hold you to that.' His laugh was strained. 'Will you be home tonight?'

She couldn't tell him tonight. She wasn't ready. Once he knew, there'd be no turning back. If he couldn't handle the idea of being a parent because it meant settling down, he'd leave Queenstown early and she would lose more time with him. 'If I do it'll be late.'

'I see.' It was clear from his voice he didn't. 'See you later in the week.'

Mallory dropped her phone back on the table with a sigh. That hadn't gone well. It didn't bode well for the discussion lying ahead of them. Would this be like before? Everything going fine with the men she fell for until the going got tough?

'Problem in the works?' Kayla asked. 'I take it that was Josue?'

'It was.' It would be too easy to spill the truth, put it out there and pick everything apart. It also wouldn't be fair, she realised. Josue deserved to be the first to know. 'I forgot he was going to pick me up for a meal before we went to the S and R meeting tonight.'

'Blame me for wanting you to stick by my side tonight.'

'I will.' Mallory picked up her orange juice and drained it. If only it had been something stronger, but then too many drinks had got her into this situation in the first place. It had to have happened the first night they'd had sex. It had been after the rescue of the two boys when she'd had a couple of beers and vodkas and hadn't thought about protection when she and Josue had got it on. 'When do you intend moving back to your house?'

'After Dad takes me in to see the surgeon next week, I'd rather hobble around on crutches in my own place. Whichever, I'm going to suggest to Josue he might as well stay on as there's not long to go before he leaves anyway.'

Mallory winced.

'If there's a problem with that I won't mention it. He can find somewhere else.'

'No, it's fine. Anyway, he's a dab hand with the mower now.' Tears streaked down her cheeks.

'Mallory?'

Josue should really be the first to know, but she needed a shoulder to cry on and she could trust Kayla not to say anything. 'I'm pregnant.'

'Come over here so I can hug you.' Kayla shuffled up the couch, awkwardly shifting her legs out of the way. 'Josue?'

Mallory nodded. 'Of course. He's leaving in a few weeks.'

'He might change his mind.'

If only it were that simple. She leaned back to look at Kayla and shook her head. 'It's going to take some work for that to happen.'

'Then you'd better get started. Tomorrow. Tonight you're staying here and we'll drink copious quantities of tea and talk just as much.'

CHAPTER SEVEN

'MALLORY, YOU'RE NEEDED to fly into the hills behind Arrowtown for a retrieval,' Pete called through from his office. 'The rescue chopper's already on an emergency flight so we're up.'

Leaping up from the desk where she'd been filling in paperwork for the tourist flights she'd done earlier in the day, she snatched up her yellow weatherproof jacket and slid into it. Funny how now she knew why she got so tired it didn't affect her as badly. 'Fill me in, boss.'

'A conservation department worker was felling trees by the Kawarau river when he slipped on unstable ground and dropped a tree on himself. He's also sliced his calf with the chainsaw. You're to fly the doctor and Jamie in to collect him and take him to Christchurch. They'll be here in five.'

Josue being the doctor? She hoped so. Even the impending news she had for him hadn't succeeded in downplaying the need he brought on, not only for the amazing sex but spending time with him, talking or not, just being in the same space. It never failed to surprise her. She'd dozed on and off throughout the night, the joy of a baby in her belly going around her head and battling with the fear it might be an ectopic pregnancy. Add Josue and what his reactions might be, and sleep hadn't got a look in. The sooner she told him the better, for both their sakes. Sara had phoned to say her scan was booked for tomorrow morning.

Mallory wouldn't relax until she'd had the scan and the result was good. But right now she had to focus on someone else and getting the man to care as soon as the men flying with her arrived. 'Who's with the forestry worker?' she asked Pete.

'Two other guys from the department. It was one of them who called for the helicopter.'

She'd tidied the chopper at the end of the last flight so all was in order. 'I'll get on board and file flight details with the tower.'

'I've flicked the coordinates through so I'll go and load the stretcher and other medical equipment for you.' Rescue gear wasn't stored on the helicopter they used for back-up emergency flights.

'Thanks,' she called.

Within minutes Mallory had the route and

destination coordinates on the screen and was pressing the button on her headset to talk to the tower. 'Queenstown Tower, Tango Juliet Romeo.'

'Come in, Tango Juliet Romeo.'

'I'm filing a flight plan for an urgent retrieval of an injured forestry worker.' She gave the co-ordinates, their estimated time of departure, number of people on board and the destination after retrieval, which today was Christchurch due to availability of theatre space and surgeon.

'Roger, Tango Juliet Romeo. We'll facilitate your departure as soon as we hear you're ready for lift-off. Over.' As Mallory sighed her relief, the air controller came back. 'Stay safe, Mallory.'

'Will do. Thanks.'

A loud thud told her the men were boarding and then the door closed. Josue popped his head through the gap between the front seats. 'We're good to go.'

She breathed deeply, taking in his presence, feeling the warmth having him near brought on. 'Great.' She began the start-up procedure. 'Want to sit up here?' she asked, without taking her eyes off the dials as they recorded pressure, heat and the increasing rotor speed reaching the levels safe for lifting off the ground. He'd get a fantastic view of the region they were going to fly over to the foothills where their patient was in dire straits, and having him there right beside her would be an added bonus, despite the problem hanging between them. It might even help break the ice.

'Love to.' Josue slid into the seat beside her and buckled up.

Sighing with relief, Mallory focused on starting the flight. Pressing the button on her mouthpiece, she gave her call sign to the tower and said, 'Ready for lift-off.'

The tower came back immediately. 'Cleared for take-off. The A320 at the west end of the runway is standing by for your clearance.'

That had been done because this was an urgent flight otherwise she'd have had to wait a few minutes after the bigger plane took off so as not to get caught in the turbulence caused by the plane's engines. 'Cleared for take-off,' Mallory repeated, as she began increasing the collective and beginning to lift the cyclic for a 40-knot attitude. 'Here we go, guys.'

Another rescue underway. Her eyes skimmed the dials in front of her, then she glanced outside, scanning the area in front of the chopper as it left the ground, moving forward and gaining altitude. Her hands firm on the controls, her mind focused on flying and looking out for dangers, her heart was tight with longing for Josue's acceptance of her and the baby.

He was interesting and exciting, dedicated to his work and when he wasn't in her bed he kept her awake late into the night with the memories of their nights together. Loving him was never going to be easy. Only now she knew those memories weren't going to be enough. She wanted to spend a lifetime making more with him. A long-distance relationship would not work, wouldn't make anyone happy long term. If she couldn't leave Queenstown then she had to find a way to tempt Josue into staying here. That should be as easy as flying the helicopter over the ranges in a blizzard. At least it was possible, she sighed.

Thinking about why Mallory had brushed him off last night and how that had hurt, even when he should've been relieved, Josue couldn't quite believe the smile she'd given him as he'd settled into his seat. He was fully aware of the helicopter lifting smoothly off the ground and rising to the approved height for their thirty-minute flight. He had no qualms about Mallory's ability to fly, even though he'd not been up in the air with her at the controls before. It was just a feeling that anything Mallory did, she did well and with complete focus. As she had on the searches they'd done together before.

He'd never thought about it before but being in an aircraft meant depending on the person or people behind the controls and today that was the woman he was coming to like and respect more and more, and to care about to the point he believed he had fallen in love. She'd got to him like no other and his heart had got involved, whether he'd wanted it to or not. He'd like nothing more than to spend all his spare time with her, be a part of the daily jobs, doing the little things that made up a full, exciting day. Could he stay permanently?

When she'd said she'd forgotten about their date last night, he hadn't believed her. There'd been something in her voice that had said there was a lot more to her being unavailable than merely forgetting. 'Why did you avoid me last night?'

'I told you. Kayla was restless. I went to spend time with her.'

'When you'd already said you'd join me for a meal before the meeting?' He wasn't buying into this.

'I didn't deliberately avoid you. I did forget we'd arranged to get together. And I forgot about the meeting.'

He had to admit she sounded genuine. 'That's

not like you.' Mallory was always organised and on the ball. 'Did you leave Shade at home too?'

'No, she came with me.' She placed a hand on his knee and squeezed lightly. 'Josue, I am really sorry for screwing up. I never meant to hurt you, I promise.'

Genuine again. It was what he wanted to hear. Had he been hasty in his reaction to her not being there for their date? Because he'd wanted to see her so badly when he was supposed to be careful? He took her hand in his and kissed her knuckles. 'Okay.'

She smiled and took her hand back to place it on the controls. 'Thanks.'

Sometimes it was still hard to believe how well they got on. The other day they'd had a wonderful time together skiing, totally in tune with each other. So much so that last night he couldn't accept she might've had a change of heart even when it would've made it easier for him to step back.

'You ready for this?' Mallory sidetracked him.

'I understand I'm to do a quick examination of the injuries, access how cognitive the patient is and decide if we need the stretcher.'

'You're on it. Hopefully it's a quick turn-around. We don't want to be hanging about too long at this time of day, and the other two on the ground still have to make their way back on foot. Luckily it's a benched track but it'll be freezing in the dark.'

Getting out of an aircraft when it wasn't on the ground always felt like a strange thing to be doing. He still didn't know what last night had been about. He understood Kayla's frustration at being stuck on the couch all the time, but not Mallory's reaction to his phone call. Was she gearing herself up for something? Did she also think that they were getting on well and that their fling was coming to mean more? Did she want to tell him she was falling for him?

He growled. This deeper sense of needing her when he couldn't guarantee to be there for her had his hands tightening into fists on his thighs. She gave him hope that he wouldn't always be alone, might finally be able to let go of some of his distrust issues. Was he hiding behind his past? Using it as an excuse to stay alone and remote and safe? If he was then Mallory unknowingly held power over him already, because the questions were rising thick and fast. Could he chance a relationship that might go further than any he'd had before? Go beyond short and fun to forever and happy? To do that he'd have to return from France with his mind fixed on letting his heart rule and not his past.

Josue shivered. If only he had the guts to

drop the past and move forward to a future that might hold all the loving scenarios he'd dreamt about as a youngster. It wasn't easy when he'd so often laid his heart on the line with foster families only to have them send him away or treat him like he wasn't there. There'd only been so many times he'd been naïve enough to believe next time would be better. Only so many times he'd let them hurt him before he'd wised up and accepted he wasn't going to find the love he needed. This was why he'd walked away from Colette and Liza. One day they'd have woken up to the fact they didn't love him. Better to get in—or in his case, out—first.

'Nearly there.' Mallory's voice came loud and clear through his headphones, reminding him they were all on a mission to save someone.

Get a grip and stop thinking about yourself. Start focusing on the rescue of a seriously injured man who needs you fully alert to his requirements. But it had been a long time since he'd got so wound up about the past and it had all started when he'd met Mallory. Throw in the job offer, and it looked like his life could come together as he wanted—if he took the chance. 'I'll go back and get prepared.'

'Get that harness ready, Josue. If we have to lower you, I don't want to be mucking around.'

Jamie hunched over and squeezed through the gap into the cockpit.

Josue slipped into the harness and altered the straps to fit snugly, twisting his shoulders left and right to make sure there were no snags. Then he got the medical pack ready to put on if they weren't landing. Excitement began streaming through his body. Rescues hyped him up as he prepared to use his skills to help someone. Add in the possibility of stepping off the side of the chopper with only a winch to keep him safe and the excitement was even greater.

'I'll return to the front and be a second pair of eyes for Mallory.'

The moment he appeared beside her she said, 'Look out your side and towards the front.' Her flat tone suggested she was concentrating on flying as much as looking for any signs of the men on the ground. It had to be a lot to contend with and she was so calm about it.

Two minutes later he pointed towards the rocky area in front of the chopper. 'There. Straight ahead.' Relief and excitement filled him as he stared at the waving men.

'Got them,' Mallory replied. 'I can't land there. I'll do a loop to see if there's somewhere close by that's clear of trees and the river.'

Immediately the helicopter banked and began turning in a wide circle. Josue could see down to the river and the high bank on one side. The other side sloped down to the water's edge but there was a lot of scrub curtailing the option of landing. As they flew round, an area of grass and rocks came into view. Would Mallory use that or were the rocks an issue? She coolly manoeuvred her machine above the up-reaching trees, her concentration completely on the job in hand.

The helicopter straightened, slowed to a hover. 'Jamie, I can put down here or we can go with lowering Josue where the men were. What do you think? Josue, did you see a way through that wouldn't be difficult with the stretcher?'

'No, I didn't.' Unfamiliar with such dense forest, he hadn't seen a track of any kind.

Jamie came back with, 'I didn't either.'

'Let's go with lowering Josue,' Jamie decided. 'Otherwise it's some haul up from the river to this spot, which won't be easy with a loaded stretcher.'

'Josue, you okay with that?' Mallory asked.

'Absolutely.' He'd begun heading into the body of the chopper but glanced back at Mallory, feeling a softness inside at her concern for him. He had the pack on his back within seconds.

Jamie attached the winch to the steel buckle on Josue's belt and checked the pack. He nodded once as he opened the door. 'As soon as you're on the ground unclip the hook. I'll lower the stretcher if required. Otherwise when you're ready to have the patient lifted let us know and raise your right arm and I'll return the winch to you. Keep us informed all the time.'

'Will do.' Josue understood it was important for everyone's sake he got this right.

'Ready?'

The helicopter was hovering above the spot they'd seen the men waving. Josue drew a breath and nodded. 'Yes.' Stepping onto the skid, one hand gripping the edge of the door, he looked down. The air whooshed out of his lungs. It wasn't a long way down, but he was going to have to step off the skid and trust the winch—and Mallory. He'd be fine. Another deep breath. 'Let's do it.'

Before he knew it, he was on the ground, with men grabbing the cable to steady him and get him unhooked. There hadn't been time to think about being in the air on the end of a cable. A smile split his face. Not bad. The noise overhead was deafening. Leaning nearer to the closest man, he shouted, 'I'm Dr Bisset. Josue.'

The guy nodded and pointed upstream towards the trees that followed the river and covered the hillside and set off.

Josue followed quickly, watching where

he placed his feet on the slippery ground. It wouldn't do to go and break an ankle now.

Then they were at the edge of the trees, where it was damp, cold and a lot darker. There was a headlight glowing at them. 'This is Russell,' he was told. 'The chainsaw went through his leg above the ankle. We figured not to remove the boot. There's a lot of damage.' The guy pulled a face.

'You did the right thing,' Josue reassured the men. The injury had been described during the call to 111 and the details passed on to him. There was a high risk the foot had been cut off, leading him to ring the hospital in Christchurch to put the surgeons on standby. 'What other injuries has he sustained? I was told the tree landed on him.'

'He's complaining of chest pain on the side and in his right arm, which he can't move. If he says he's hurting, then he's in agony. He's a tough bastard at the best of times.'

Josue refrained from pointing out the obvious and knelt down beside the man they'd just reached. 'Hello, Russell. I'm Josue, a doctor. We're going to get you out of here fairly quickly but first I need to check you over.'

'Just do what you have to,' Russell grunted.

Josue looked at the boot-clad foot. What was

left of the boot was helping slow the bleeding. He'd leave it in place. There was nothing he could do to improve the situation out here anyway. Once on board he'd apply tight bandages to help keep the blood flow to a minimum. From what he could see, he didn't like the chances of it being saved, but who knew? Surgeons could work miracles given half a chance. 'What's under that strapping?' he asked over his shoulder. The lower leg had been bound with what appeared to be a shirt torn into strips.

'Russ was bleeding all along the calf muscle up to the knee so we did what we could to stop it,' one of the men answered.

'You've done an excellent job looking after him.' At least Russell's neck and spine appeared to be uninjured by the way he was moving his head and shoulders, though Josue suspected the movement would be causing him some pain. 'Stay still if you can.'

'Reckon the arm's broken. My ribs hurt a bit too.'

Interpret 'a bit' to mean hurt like hell, Josue mused as he carefully felt along the ulna and radius of Russell's right arm. 'Movement won't be helping either your arm or your ribs.' Under his fingers he felt an inconsistency on the bones. 'You've fractured both bones in your lower arm.

I'm going to look at your chest. Tell me about the pain there.'

'Only when I breathe too deep. Reckon that frigging tree got me fair and square.'

'I know this will hurt but take a long slow breath for me.' With a stethoscope Josue listened to Russell's lungs and heart. 'Good. You can stop. You may have broken some ribs but your lungs haven't been ruptured.' He pressed the button on his headset. 'Jamie, we need the stretcher.'

'On its way.'

'How's it going down there, Josue?' Mallory's voice was soft in his ears, and he smiled.

Impossible to stay distant with her when his heart went soft when she was near. 'All good. We'll be out of here shortly. The sooner our man's in hospital the better.' Still smiling, he said to the men with him, 'Can you get the stretcher?'

'On my way,' one of them answered.

'Right. Russell, I'm going to give you a shot of painkiller before we haul you up and on board.'

'Would prefer a bourbon,' the man croaked.

'You can pretend I'm giving you one intravenously,' Josue joked as he filled the syringe. He hoped this tough guy could weather what lay ahead with as much nonchalance.

* * *

'They're ready.' Jamie's voice came through the headset.

Mallory brought the helicopter over the men on the ground and slowly descended to ten metres, then hovered. 'Go.' Looking down, she saw Josue standing bent over his patient, protecting the man from the downdraught. Her heart softened for his kindness. She'd seen others do the same thing but from what he'd said Josue hadn't had much experience with chopper rescues and yet doing the right thing by his patient seemed to come naturally. Yeah, he was a good bloke, as the guys in the search and rescue crews would say. But she already knew that.

She read the dials, checked everything was as it should be, looked out and around the location and nodded. All good. The sky was beginning to darken but they'd be well on the way to Christchurch before night took over completely. At least it would be all twinkling stars as the weather forecast was for minus six in the morning. No wind or rain this end of the South Island, but watch out on Saturday. Storms bringing snow and ice were predicted. She shivered at the thought.

'Coming up now,' Jamie warned.

Keeping a firm eye on everything, she waited to be told everyone was on board. The man had to be in a serious condition. When a chainsaw was involved it usually meant horrendous injuries, and then a tree had fallen on top of him too. The injuries wouldn't be pretty.

A light thump, then the winch was dropping the cable down again to Josue.

Leaning against her window, she glanced down at the man who had her longing for things she shouldn't. Josue was attaching the hook that would haul him up, looking well at ease. Why did *he* make her think about love and a long-term relationship? Why not the last guy she'd spent time getting to know, only to decide he wasn't worth the effort?

She hadn't felt this sense of having found someone worth putting everything into, of risking her heart again, in a long time. Not since Hogan, and he'd been quite different, expecting her to change to fit in with him all the time. Josue took her for who she was, and didn't knock her faults. Of course this was early days, when everything was generally rosy, but somehow she didn't think Josue was going to turn out to be a very different man from the one she was slowly—but surely—falling deeper and deeper in love with. Come on, there hadn't been anything slow about it at all. *More like slam, bang, here I am.* She sighed.

Josue had disappeared from sight below the

chopper, meaning he'd be on board in a second. Mallory dragged her attention back to what was important right at this moment and focused on being ready to ascend the moment Jamie said they were set.

Josue would spend the flight caring for the injured man, utterly focused on watching for bleeding, making certain the man's breathing was all right and that his heart wasn't faltering, administering pain relief that wasn't going to affect being taken to Theatre for surgery. She knew all this from previous flights with other doctors. He would not come forward and sit beside her to Christchurch, but he might on the way back to Queenstown.

In the meantime, she'd make sure they had a fast but safe trip. 'All set,' Jamie called. He would watch Josue and help wherever he could. That was Jamie. She'd worked with him on enough rescues to know he was always sucking up information, learning what he could as often as opportunities arose. When she thought about it, he and Josue had a lot in common.

'Russell, open your eyes. Look at me.' Josue's sharp command came through the headset and she could hear his worry, like there was a problem going on.

Better not be, Mallory thought. *Our team doesn't like bad results. They cause despair and sleepless nights.* Turning the helicopter in the direction of the river, she flew downstream, ascending until she reached a safe height, and then headed for Canterbury and the hospital in Christchurch, one ear listening out for Josue.

'That's it, Russell. You're in the helicopter and we're flying to Christchurch. Understand?' A pause. 'Good.' Some of the tension had left Josue's voice.

Mallory relaxed. If Josue was comfortable with how his patient was doing, then she was content with flying them all to get help. She hated the trips that were touch and go every minute of the way. She felt pressured to push harder than was safe. Not that she ever did but she couldn't help wondering how she'd feel if that was someone she loved back there with serious injuries.

On today's flight there *was* a man in the back she was keen on. She'd spent a lot of nights with him in her bed now and still wanted more. Her hand slid over her belly. A lot more. Her rare flings had never amounted to more than a few exciting moments before they'd finished, no hard feelings.

Initially that's what she'd hoped she'd started with Josue, despite the niggling feeling that there was more to him than other men she'd dated. As the days had gone by she'd realised she wanted to be with him as much as possible and not only in bed or on rescues. Now there was a baby in the mix. She held her breath, searching for pain in her abdomen and finding none. Bring on the scan and hopefully she could drop this fear that was even stronger than telling Josue he might become a father.

'Feel up to some dinner?' Josue asked from right beside her seat in the chopper parked outside the hangar in Queenstown.

Mallory tugged her eyes open and turned to look at him. Looked right into those eyes filled with wariness. Dang, she was tired. 'Sounds good,' she said through a yawn. Flying to Christchurch and back had taken every last drop of her concentration.

'Sorry to wake you up.'

'Yeah, I know. It's hard to get any peace around here.' Even her smile felt tired. 'I wanted a few minutes to myself. I always do after a rescue flight.' She needed to remember the patient was in good hands and had been all the time. Needed to accept she'd done her best and couldn't have done anything more. Needed to let go and get on with the rest of her night.

'I get like that too,' Josue admitted.

'Where do you want to eat? I'd prefer to stay at home.' Right now, going home and heating something from the freezer was as much as she could contemplate. Pregnancy was turning her into a dull old woman.

His hand covered her shoulder, squeezed gently. 'No problem. I'll sort some food. Let's get out of here.'

Did this mean she was forgiven for last night? 'I'll finish checking over the helicopter and sign off the paperwork and then head home.'

'I'll see you there in a bit.' His smile looked as tired as hers felt, and he still held himself back a little.

A shower. That's what she needed to ease the kinks in her back and warm away the tiredness in her muscles. *'Merci.'* That and *oui* were about the only French words she knew. Might be time to learn some more. Like *touch me. Kiss me.* 'See you when you're ready.' Learn to say I love you. You're going to be a father. *If* this pregnancy was normal.

Josue leaned in close and kissed her cheek. 'You *were* great today.'

'Just doing my job.' She loved her job and put everything into it. Hopefully she'd be able to fly for a while before the baby got in the way. If the baby wasn't in her fallopian tube. Thud. Her heart stuttered. Tomorrow would reveal the answer she was desperate for. The right answer. Her teeth were sharp, digging into her bottom lip.

'Doing it exceptionally well, or so it seemed for someone not very experienced with being in a helicopter. And stop chewing your lip. I'll feed you, I promise.'

If only he knew. He could, if she got on with telling him. *Tonight?* Yes, it had to be. There was no reason not to, and it would be good if he could go to the scan with her, though he was probably working tomorrow. 'See you soon.'

Breathing deep, inhaling a combination of Josue and aviation fuel, she got on with the checks required at the end of every flight, aware of Josue as he chattered with Jamie in the back as they packed the stretcher and gathered their gear before leaving the aircraft.

Just hearing his accent had her tummy tightening like a small caress. Then she recalled him whispering in French against her skin during the nights they'd spent together and the caress became thick with heat and need. *You've got it bad, Mallory.* Yep, she did. Only one thing to do about that. Enjoy every minute she had, making the most of him while she could and to heck with worrying about what to do when he left because no amount of fretting could change anything.

If only it was that simple. She hoped he didn't

walk away from the life-changing news she was about to load on him. She didn't believe he would. No, make that she didn't *want* to believe he would. Josue took responsibility seriously, and this was his child, but he didn't do stopping in one place long term. He had a lot of fears to overcome. She'd do everything possible to help him through those. That's what love was about. She'd seen it with her parents, the support and unbreakable love that had got them through miscarriages and loss of jobs, and knew that's what she would give Josue. If he'd accept her being a part of his life. *If*—such a small word, so many directions it could go.

She crossed her fingers and yawned. Damn, she was exhausted. She was more likely to fall asleep at the table tonight than talk to Josue about the future.

CHAPTER EIGHT

SHADE MET JOSUE at the door, tail wagging and her nose raised to the pizzas he carried in one hand.

'No, girl, they're not for you.' He tried to ignore the hope shining up at him but Shade didn't make it easy. 'Even if you are gorgeous.'

'Shade, behave. You've been fed.' Mallory stood at the other end of the short hallway with a wide but tired grin on her face. 'You're such a sucker for those big eyes, Doctor.'

Forget Shade's beguiling eyes. It was the pair watching him that were devouring him with warmth. Josue's mouth dried. Mallory was heart-wrenchingly pretty. Dressed in a white floaty blouse that had a light blue floral pattern that matched the blue on her nails and fitted rust-coloured trousers that were feminine and accentuated her shape to perfection, she had him in the palm of her hand.

Her wavy hair shone under the light and

had his hand itching to touch it. She'd put on new make-up, a little more accentuated than what she'd worn to work. This was Mallory the woman away from the predominantly male environment she worked in. 'You look beautiful.' Nothing to do with the make-up either.

She blinked, shook her head and looked away.

So there was still something bothering her.

Then her focus returned to him, a crimson shade colouring her cheeks. 'Are you going to stand there all night?'

'You think?' Since both hands were full he closed the door with his heel and followed her into the family room, where she'd laid out plates. 'Do you like Pinot noir, by any chance?' He'd stopped in at the supermarket while waiting for the pizzas.

'I do, but then I like most wines. Central Otago's well known for Pinot noirs.'

'Just as well I bought a local brand then.'

Placing the bottle and the pizzas on the table, he went into the kitchen and took glasses out of the cupboard. He was so comfortable here, as though he'd always been doing this. He knew where everything was, and how Mallory liked things to look. He'd brought her a large bunch of roses the second week he'd visited her here and had replaced them every week since because she got so much pleasure out a simple

gesture that he did from the bottom of his heart.
He'd started believing he could make settling
down work, that the urge to run whenever the
going got rough might not rear up so quickly,
and when it did that he'd be able to manage it.

When Mallory hadn't turned up last night,
he'd begun to feel the pain that losing her would
bring and already the shutters had started to
come down over his heart. The old need to go
before she kicked him out had begun ringing
loud and clear, reminding him how he usually
did things.

His reasoning had been about going home
for Gabriel, when in truth if he wasn't afraid of
rejection he'd surely find a way to make everything work. He couldn't necessarily offer secu-
rity to Mallory but he could try his hardest. If
she wanted it. Why would she? She was confident in her own life.

Despite the love for her slowly expanding in
his chest that he desperately wanted to follow,
so was the fear of rejection. It was bigger than
before, which told him his feelings for her were
also bigger than he'd ever experienced before.
The time to make a firm decision to move forward or step back was rushing at him with an
incomprehensible speed. As much as he loved
her, he still didn't trust himself to do the right
thing by both of them.

'Josue?' She was right beside him.

'Let's eat. I'm starving.' For a lot of things. That's what was leading him into trouble. He couldn't let Mallory go, and yet sooner or later he might have to. He *was* leaving. He had to be there for Gabriel's operation so it would be safer to walk away from her while he still could, in case he wasn't coming back. *If* he could. He had yet to tell John his decision. He knew he was stalling. Since when had he got so indecisive? Since his heart had got involved.

'Me too.' Mallory was watching him with a big question in her eyes. 'Will you stay the night?'

That wasn't what was darkening those eyes but he'd go with it for now. He rubbed her back where she often ached after flying. *'Oui.'* His answer had come instinctively from the heart. How could he not spend another night with Mallory? Could he make this the last one? Impossible. *Grow a backbone. You want to look out for her, you've got to make up your mind and stick to it. One way or the other.*

'Are you working tomorrow?' Mallory had moved away to sit at the table and open the pizza boxes, sniffing the air like a hound.

He'd never eaten so many pizzas, and they weren't even a favourite. Another example of Mallory getting to him. 'I've got two days off.

Two whole days in succession.' Might be an idea to go away somewhere, stay overnight in another town, do some sightseeing in the name of giving himself some space from his heart's desire.

'What are you going to do with them?'

Quickly thinking of the places he'd been told were must-sees, he went with, 'I thought I'd drive to Fiordland and go for a boat trip. I hear it's quite something.' He sat opposite her and lifted the wine bottle. 'Yes?'

'Yes to dinner. No to wine tonight. It's late and it'll keep me awake.'

'That's the idea.' He smiled and filled one glass. 'You're sure you won't have a little?'

'No, thanks.' She got up to get a glass of water, sat back down and reached for some food.

Needing to fill the gap in conversation before he blurted something awkward, like he wanted to spend more time with her, he said, 'Sometime before I head home I'd like to see the albatross colony at Dunedin. That's more interesting to me than Larnach's Castle. Not saying it wouldn't be interesting but we have plenty of castles in France.'

'Far grander, I'd expect.' Mallory was chewing slowly and her gaze seemed fixed on the family photos hanging on the wall behind him. What was she thinking about?

'What's up?'

Shaking her head, abruptly she bit into her pizza. 'Nothing.'

He never believed her when she said nothing, but he didn't want to argue. He'd done enough arguing with himself to last the week. They finished up dinner and cleared away the dishes in a companionable yet not completely relaxed silence.

Then Mallory made herself tea and said, 'I'm taking this to bed. You joining me?'

'I'll take Shade for a quick walk first, shall I?' The dog had grown restless in the last few minutes. Mallory always took her along the road or around the lawn before she settled down for the night so it seemed odd she was going to bed straight away.

'Would you? I'm exhausted.'

When Josue and Shade returned to the house, he was surprised to find Mallory sitting on the couch, drinking her tea and flicking idly through a magazine. Warmth spread through him. This was just how he imagined couples to be. Sharing the chores, making everything easier for each other and then going to bed and making love. He sighed. He adored Mallory. It no longer shocked him that he felt this way. It was true. He woke most mornings with happiness coursing through his veins and hope for another wonderful day in his heart. Mallory had given him this. Leaning over, he brushed his lips over her forehead. Maybe he could make it work for them.

'I thought you were going to bed.' There were shadows under her eyes, and when he thought about it, they'd been there all day. Hadn't she been sleeping well? Had the tension between them not really disappeared and was causing her to lie awake at night? Had he wanted to believe her so much when she'd apologised for missing their date that he'd avoided hearing something he might not like? Something different to what he'd begun hoping for? He hoped not. 'What's going on?'

Silence answered him.

'The only time you've been distant with me was when you forgot our date yesterday.' He highlighted 'forgot' with his forefingers.

Her shoulders tensed. She was scratching at her trousers above her knee. Not a Mallory action at all. Unless she was worried. Then she looked up and faced him squarely. 'Josue, sit down.'

The last time someone had spoken to him like that had been when he'd been about to be kicked out of school. He folded his arms across his chest and leaned his backside against the back of an armchair. 'What's going on?'

If only they could go to her bedroom and make love, sleep spooned together and then in the morning get up and share breakfast before Josue got organised for a day in Fiordland.

Mallory breathed deeply. That wasn't happening. There'd be no sleeping for her until he knew, and probably none afterwards. She couldn't have one last night when the baby didn't come between them because it was already there, causing trouble for their relationship.

Once Josue knew, nothing would be quite the same. Naturally he'd be shocked, just as she had been. But for Josue there was so much more to contend with. His past would be a big part of how he reacted. He wasn't going to sweep her up into his arms and tell her it was the most amazing news he'd ever heard and that the three of them would make a great family, even if he wanted to. Not Josue.

She was going to have to be patient and support him while waiting, impatiently, with crossed fingers. She loved him, and for her that meant one thing: together forever, loving each other and their child.

'Mallory, what is going on?' he demanded

in a voice she didn't recognise. Was he getting angry with her?

Pulling her eyes open, she stared into Josue's troubled gaze and bit her lip hard to stop herself from crying. He was the most wonderful man she'd ever known, and any minute now she was probably going to lose him forever.

'Talk to me.'

Wriggling deeper into the couch, she gave him a weak smile. Talk to him? *Yes, Josue, that's exactly what I'm about to do. I hope you'll still be able to hug me afterwards.* 'You...' Gulp. 'I...'

Worry was darkening that steady gaze. 'What about us?' He didn't blink, didn't move a finger, his breathing was tight.

I can do this. 'Josue, I'm pregnant.'

Silence answered her.

Shock widened his eyes, tightened his mouth, but he said nothing, didn't cross to touch her, didn't move further away. Nothing.

She waited, breathless, stomach knotted, heart barely beating. And waited.

Finally, 'Is that why you've been so tired?'

Of all the things she'd guessed he might say, that wasn't one of them. He'd put his doctor's cap on. 'I think so. Plus the fact I'm terrified I could have another ectopic pregnancy has kept me from sleeping these last couple of nights.'

'Another? You've been pregnant before?'

'I was eighteen. My boyfriend left me at the time. I'm having a scan tomorrow to make sure this pregnancy is all right.'

Josue winced. 'How long have you known?'

'I found out yesterday, which was why I forgot about the meeting.'

His arms unfolded and lined up with his sides. His gaze was still directed on her. 'You didn't think to tell me then?'

She stood up, moved closer. Reaching for his hand, she wound hers around it. 'I wanted to tell you, but I needed to get everything clear in my mind.'

His hand jerked away. 'Everything? Like what exactly?'

She'd known this wasn't going to be easy but it still hurt. At the moment Josue was turning everything back on her. Probably his way of working through the shock of learning he was going to be a father. She would give him time to get used to the idea. 'Firstly, I want this baby very much.'

Josue's arms went back across his chest, his fingers white against his green jersey. 'I'd have been stunned if you thought otherwise.'

That was a positive sign, wasn't it? Did he feel the same? 'Family is important to me. I'm sure it's the same for you.'

'I don't talk about how I've always done my utmost not to be in this position because, as you know, I don't stay around long enough to be a parent.'

Her shoulders sagged. *Here we go.* She waited to hear him out.

'I can't give a child—or a partner—the stable life they deserve. How can I when I haven't had the experience of a loving family?' He shoved both hands through his hair, leaving it sticking up on end. 'This is crazy.'

'I couldn't fly a helicopter until I was taught.' She glared at him. *Easy, girl. He's taking this hard.* 'You learned to be a doctor, Josue. You can learn to be a fantastic father. And partner. Think what Gabriel and his wife gave you, how they shared their lives to help you make yours better.'

Josue stared at her as though he didn't recognise her. 'You think so?' He snapped his fingers. 'Just like that they wiped away my fears and pain? I spent my younger life being rejected, only to turn it around so now I do the rejecting. Does that sound like an ideal partner or father?'

'What I know is that my parents raised me with love and care. They taught me to be who I am. I am going to do the same with our child. We can do this, you and I.'

'No, Mallory. You don't know what you're saying. You really don't.'

'You're about to walk out on us?' She was going for the jugular, but being tough was in her blood, and Josue was worth every bit of her strength. She was resilient and would not let him go easily. He needed to understand she'd be there every time he tripped, as he would be for her if he gave them half a chance.

'No, Mallory, I'm going to go along the road to my bedroom to do a whole lot of thinking. I cannot guarantee you or any child a settled life, living with me.' Suddenly he blinked. Tears appeared in his eyes.

'Josue, you don't have to leave next month.' Damn, she'd all but begged there. That wouldn't help her case. 'Your visa has another year to run.'

'Yes, Mallory, I do. I promised Gabriel I'd be there for his surgery.'

'What are you talking about?' Her heart started banging hard. This might mean she'd never stood a chance of winning Josue over.

'He's having a coronary bypass. It was meant to happen in June but he got flu so it was delayed until next month. It's not urgent but his surgeon wants to do it while he's still in relatively good health. After all Gabriel and Brigitte have done for me I have to be there for them. I *am* their surrogate son.' A tight squeeze of her hand and he was back on his feet and reaching for his phone. 'Goodnight, Mallory.'

It sounded like goodbye. 'Wait. Of course you have to be with Gabriel and Brigitte. I understand, but you can come back afterwards.'

'Have you heard a thing I've said?'

Despite his denial, she dredged up a weak smile. 'Yes, I have. All of it, and here's the thing. I believe in you.' Her heart spilled into her words.

He glared at her. 'Laying it on a bit thick, aren't you?'

'It's the only way to get through to you.'

'Believe me, you did that with the words "I'm pregnant". They're going round and round in my head like a broken record.'

Josue was a kind, gentle man who wanted love. Did he not realise how much he loved the couple who'd taken him in and that if he loved them so much, he could love others? Especially his child? And if only he could love her, then they'd have no problems with this.

'I'll see you later on.' He was at the door, looking at her as though he'd forgotten why he'd been here in the first place.

He doesn't love me. The thought slammed into her, took her breath away and stopped her heart. Her hands splayed across her abdomen.

Sorry, baby, but Daddy doesn't love Mummy. I love him, though. With everything I have. Josue needed to know that. If he threw it back in her face, she'd falter, but she'd stand tall, take the hurt on the chin, and fight for him. What a disaster this was turning out to be. He held on to his feelings too tightly. But he had been relaxing more and more, becoming a part of her life. She'd never told him her feelings for him either.

'Josue, wait.' She raced down the hall and out onto the porch. 'There's something you need to know.'

'Something more?'

She strode up to him and looked into those sad, lonely eyes. 'I love you with all my heart, Josue. You, and only you.'

He swayed towards her, then straightened, all the while looking at her, as though trying to find if she was being honest.

She said it again, with all her heart in every word. 'I love you.'

Then he was gone, stepping quietly along the footpath towards the house he wouldn't be staying in much longer.

I love you.

Mallory's words echoed in Josue's head again and again as he strode up to Kayla's house. He believed her. No one had ever said that to him before, not as clear and unadorned. Not even the two people who'd taken him under their wing.

'I love you.'

He tasted the words, listened to them, breathed them in. They scared him. They warmed him, undermined his worry about not being good enough for Mallory or their child.

A baby. He was going to be a father. Him. Who didn't know the first thing about raising a child with his heart. As a doctor he knew all too well how to change a soiled nappy or feed a hungry tot. As a man—he needed a manual and that was hardly the way to go about it.

Letting himself into the house, he flicked lights on and stared around at Kayla's home, so unlike Mallory's warm comfortable place that had caught his breath the first time he'd opened her front door. He couldn't stay another night here when Kayla was Mallory's best friend. He was the odd one out. Did Kayla know about the baby? They'd had been together last night. Kayla had told him on the phone she was returning home and that he could stay on for the rest of his time here.

Right now he needed to get away from Mallory's friend's space, from Mallory down the road. He'd head into town to find a hotel room for the night. Or he could hit the road and head to Fiordland, get there before the sun rose. Except the last thing he felt like doing now was being a sightseer. There was more than enough to look at inside his head.

In the bedroom he sank onto the bed and tried to decide what to do, but all that came to mind was walking back down the road and climbing into bed with Mallory, to hug her and never let go. Which was irresponsible. He had to make some decisions before anything else.

He was going to be a dad. Yes. Incredible. Unbelievable. To think parenthood had never been a part of his thinking and yet here he was, a father-to-be, with the only woman he'd loved so deeply she had him looking at who he was and who he might become if he found the guts to do it. How was it that the deeper the difficulties the more he found he loved her?

Why not go to her now and say that? Express his love in words. He'd been showing her in small ways, but she needed to hear him say it. So did he. Except he knew if he opened his mouth the only thing that would come out was his fear of failing her, or her rejecting him. He'd tell her he was leaving.

She said she loved you.

He had to go. Grabbing a bag, he tossed in all

his gear, locked up the house, put the key back in the meter box, and drove away, slowing as he passed Mallory's house, which was in darkness. *Bet she's not sleeping.*

I love you, Josue.

'And I love you, Mallory, but that doesn't mean I won't hurt you.'

In town, Josue pulled up by the lake's edge, got out and started walking. It was easy going with a full moon to light his way. He wasn't tired. Not enough to go to sleep anyway.

He might never sleep again if he didn't sort this out.

What was his problem? Apart from his fear of letting Mallory and his baby down? Of being rejected despite her claim to love him? Wasn't that enough? She'd said he could do this, but she didn't know how little he knew. She was wrong to believe in him. He had warned her.

Bending down, he picked up a handful of pebbles and one at a time threw them across the calm water to bounce again and again before disappearing underneath the surface. Like him: he bounced along, meeting women, getting to know them, liking them, and then he sank, leaving only circles of emptiness behind him.

He was about to do that to Mallory.

Turning back the way he had come, his steps

were slow. What if he went to the scan with her? Supported her? And then walked away?

That would be worse than not showing up at all.

The scan was important for her. The pain in her face when she'd mentioned the ectopic pregnancy had hit him hard. If this was another of those she'd be devastated. Someone should be with her. If she didn't ask Kayla to go with her, he should. He was in a relationship with Mallory, no matter how hard he tried to look the other way, especially if she carried the baby to full term. They had made this baby together.

If Mallory believed he could do this, then he had to believe in himself. She'd been fierce when telling him they could make it work. Then she'd been so close to tears when she'd said she loved him. Those tears had nearly undone him and had him on his knees, begging for her to take him on, fears and all.

What? Josue scooped up some more pebbles and began flicking them across the surface. *He wanted this child?* Splash. Yes, he did—if he could guarantee him or her a happy, loving life. One where he was always there, always encouraging and supporting.

It wouldn't happen. He would be doing Mallory and the child a favour by getting out of here sooner rather than later, and never, ever coming back or making contact.

He turned back to his vehicle and began driving out of town.

Early the next morning Mallory sat in her car, afraid to put the key in the ignition because the moment she started the engine her journey to the scanning wand would begin.

She couldn't bear to think this might be the last opportunity to be pregnant, to have a baby.

'Stop being negative,' Kayla had growled over the phone last night before offering to go to Invercargill with her. 'The doctor told you everything appeared normal.'

'I'm afraid to believe her,' Mallory had admitted. After all, she had hoped there was a chance Josue would believe her when she told him she loved him. Round three in the love stakes had stabbed her in the heart and was even more debilitating than the previous two. She was on her own in this. Kayla and Maisie would be there for her any time she called for help, but *if* she was going to be a mother then she had to stand tall and strong right from the get-go. It might be the only chance she got and there was no way she was going to get it wrong.

She'd put on heavier than usual make-up to put some colour in her white cheeks and cover the dark shadows below her eyes. It had been a long, sleepless night as hope that Josue might love her faded to despair as reality returned. He'd been stunned by her declaration, but there hadn't been any love coming her way, only bewilderment and fear. Plus the need to get away from her. That had hurt, but she had been warned.

There was a light tapping on her window.

Looking out, she gasped. 'Josue?' She stared at him. He looked as dishevelled as she felt. What did he want? She had to get on the road. Pressing the button, she opened the window. 'Hello.'

'You look like you had about as much sleep as I did. That's not the way to look after yourself, Mallory.'

If that's all he'd come to say, he could go away. 'You think?' She wouldn't mention not being able to force a single mouthful of toast down her throat for breakfast, and that only tea had made it past the lump in her throat, and then not a whole mug full.

'I'm coming with you.'

'Really? Just like that?' She ignored the hope rising inside her chest. It might mean nothing more than he needed to see proof that she was pregnant. Anger began winding her up. He'd come along for his own sake and nothing to do with how she might feel. Then he'd pack up and leave town. 'I don't think so, Josue. This is more than a quick squizz at a scan to see if I am safely pregnant and not going to have a procedure to remove my last Fallopian tube.' This was about her future, whether he was a part of that or not.

'I understand.'

'Do you?'

'Honestly? I'm trying.'

She stared at him long and hard, trying to sort through all the worries slapping around her skull, but there were too many and she was already exhausted. There was a long drive ahead too. 'Get in.'

'Want me to drive?'

Her shoulders slumped. So much for being strong. 'Yes, please.'

Josue opened the door and helped her out of the seat, led her around to the passenger side. Like she was an invalid.

She swallowed that one. They were going to be crammed into her car for a while, no point in getting grouchy. As they buckled themselves in she tried for normal, and asked, 'Where did you spend the night?'

Josue's car hadn't been parked outside Kayla's house when the sun had come up.

'I've moved out of the house.'

If she'd thought there was any hope at all by

his turning up to go with her to Invercargill it had just taken a dive. He *was* leaving.

'Warm enough?' he asked as he started up the car.

'Yes.'

'Where are we going for this scan?'

'Invercargill Hospital.'

Josue stopped asking questions and Mallory sank down and closed her eyes. There was so much to say but she wasn't in the mood. All she wanted was to know her baby was where it should be and was going to be fine. Whatever Josue would do had to come second for now.

CHAPTER NINE

'ARE YOU COMING in with me?' Mallory asked as Josue parked outside the hospital. It had been a silent trip.

'Do you want me to?'

'Josue, answer the bloody question, will you?' She vented her frustration. 'What do you want?'

'To be there for you.' He wasn't looking at her.

Did this baby mean nothing to him? Or was this his fear taking control? Well, she'd decided to fight for him. Might as well start now. 'Thank you. I'd like your company, especially if…' She swallowed, unable to go on.

Now he faced her, nothing but concern in his expression. 'One step at a time, Mallory.'

Was that how he was dealing with all this? One step at a time? She'd ignore the tiny bubble of hope that brought on. 'Let's go in.'

Half an hour later, after waiting for the scan and then having the wand run across the goo on her abdomen, Mallory held her breath and stared at the radiologist.

A broad smile on his face brought her another bubble of hope. 'Mallory, Josue, all is well. Your baby is where it should be and looking as it's meant to. That's about all I can say at this stage. But you can stop worrying about an ectopic pregnancy.'

'All is well.' The statement bounced around Mallory's head. *My baby's real. This is really happening.* Her heart was bubbling fit to burst. She was going to be a mother. Bring him or her on.

'That's wonderful.'

Josue. Mallory blinked, looked to him and saw relief mixed with bewilderment coming at her. He didn't know where this left him. He hadn't made any decisions. Swallowing her disappointment, she reached for his hand and held tight. 'Yes, it is. Thank you, Doctor. I've been so scared and now I feel as though I'm walking on air.'

'I understand. I'm glad to have been the bearer of good news.' His eyes flicked to Josue and a frown appeared on his brow. 'I'll leave you both to absorb everything. A copy of the result will be sent to your GP.'

Just like that they were alone in the small space. Mallory shivered in the suddenly chill air. 'Josue, come on. Let's get outside and back on the road.'

'Yes, of course. What a relief for you.'

For me? 'It is the absolute best result I could get.' Her pregnancy really was normal. Phew. Unbelievable. Exciting. She clapped her hands. 'Fantastic.'

Josue said nothing.

'What about you? Does this make you happy?' She watched him think up an answer.

'I was thinking how worried you were this might be a repeat. I am very happy that you're not going through that again.'

'That sounds as though you've decided you're definitely having nothing to do with us. You're heading home, never to return.'

'Is that what I said?' His head shot up, and he locked a fierce look on her.

That was so out of character that she knew she'd gone too far. But she was fighting for him, for the father of her baby and for the man she loved and wanted to spend the rest of her life with. 'You haven't said anything. That's the trouble, Josue. I'd like to know what you're going to do.' Her hands were clenched. 'Sooner rather than later.'

'I'm sorry.' He looked the other way while she got back into her clothes, then took her elbow and started towards the lift that'd take them down to the car park. 'Let's wait until we're on our own before finishing this.'

Finishing this? Not starting or continuing, but finishing. The thrill at learning her baby was safe had been shunted aside with the dread that Josue was leaving them. Knowing how likely that was didn't make this any easier to accept. It'd have been better not to get her hopes up but she'd already given herself that speech weeks ago and hadn't managed to keep him at a distance. She loved him with everything she had and nothing would change that. No amount of pleading, telling him she loved him, asking him to reconsider would change his stubborn mind once he'd made it up.

Outside she waited for Josue to say something.

Instead he headed for the car, head down against the sharp wind, and his hand still on her elbow as though she needed support.

It would've been childish to pull away so she upped her pace to keep up and pretended the slight pressure from his fingers was loving.

Inside the car he turned on the heater and started for the main road back to Queenstown, his shoulders tight as he drove. His lips pressed against each other and his eyes were dark.

Did she give him a break or push for his thoughts?

She leaned back, her hand touching her stomach. A wave of happiness rolled through her, quickly gone. But she'd felt it, knew it to be true. Now that she could relax about an ectopic pregnancy not being a problem she was thrilled about the baby. One step on the way to her future was underway. Funny how when she hadn't been looking for it, it had happened anyway. Now she had Josue to talk to and make him see her love meant helping him overcome his difficulties and be happy too. 'Josue…'

Josue drew a breath. 'I've been offered a permanent position at the hospital with help to get a resident's visa should I want one.'

Her mouth fell open. Obviously she hadn't seen that coming. Why would she have? He'd kept quiet about everything going on in his life.

'Is that a good thing?' she asked.

'I'm still headed to Nice next month.'

'Even now you know about the baby?'

'I don't make rash decisions.' Even to him that sounded like he was covering up his feelings. Which he probably was.

She snapped, 'Rash stopped when I got pregnant.'

'Mallory, it may be straightforward for you to accept you're having a baby, but as I've never contemplated the idea…' He hesitated. Even if he hadn't, how could he not be excited knowing he was going to be a father? First he'd fallen in love, then been offered a job that fitted in with being with Mallory and now they were having a baby. It was too much to take in. It was so far out of his norm he was stumbling. 'You know my story.'

'Tell me more. There're a lot of gaps.'

'I've never considered being a parent and now I've been confronted with the fact that I might have to without a say in the matter.'

'Like me, you mean?' She didn't look at him, just sat watching the kilometres disappearing under the front of the car.

'I suppose it is exactly the same, regardless of our different backgrounds.'

'Background has nothing to do with this.' Breathing deep, she asked softly, 'Then tell me what you're going to do. Stay or go?'

If only it was that straightforward. Josue braked as a truck cut across his line of traffic. Pressing his palm on the horn, he yelled, 'Idiot.'

Mallory looked across to him. 'Easy.'

Which only made him madder. How could he take anything easy when she wanted answers about the future? Wanted commitment from him? More than anything he wanted to tell her he was here forever, would raise their child with her, would buy a house and settle down and get everything right. If only he could say the words 'I love you' without tripping over them, without doubting them. 'Sure.'

He concentrated on driving and let the tension grow because he didn't know how to stop it without letting years of worry explode out of him. His knuckles were white, his stomach tighter than a basketball. To let rip would drive a wedge between them that could take years to fix. Not the way to get into a permanent relationship or to welcome a child into the world. If he was actually going to do it, and he still did not know the answer to that. The doubts far outweighed everything else.

Somewhere during the ride back to Queenstown, Mallory fell asleep. Josue relaxed a little and glanced across at her regularly. Tiredness lined her face but the fear of losing her baby had gone, leaving her as beautiful as ever. *'Je t'adore,'* he said quietly. 'But I doubt it's enough to walk into your life and never leave.'

At her house he went and unlocked the door then returned to lift her out and carried her into the bedroom, where he laid her on the bed and pulled a cover over her. 'Bye, Mallory.'

Whether she heard him he had no idea, but she didn't move or blink so he guessed not. Which meant she'd probably be annoyed when she woke up and found herself alone at home.

But as he stepped out of her room he heard a call.

'Josue? Are you there?'

Returning, he stood at the edge of her bed. *Don't ask me anything. I do not want to answer questions I have no idea about.* 'You've been out for the count most of the trip. I thought it best to let you continue sleeping.'

She wasn't buying it. 'Dodging the bullets?'

Leaning closer, he tucked a stray strand of hair behind her ear and locked his eyes on hers. 'For now, yes. I have some calls to make. All right?'

She stared at him as though searching deep inside for the truth. Finally Mallory gave him a small smile. 'I guess.'

His legs were shaky as he stepped away. He didn't want to leave her even for an hour but he had to. He was not making any promises he could not keep. Neither was he going to let loose the anger that he'd been holding in all the way back from Invercargill. 'See you later.' *Maybe.*

Not having sorted new accommodation yet, he drove to the same spot by the lake and parked. After staring at the water for a long time he got out and strode along the water's edge again. The water calmed him, as did the view of Cecil's Peak on the other side of the lake. This was a beautiful place and he could see himself living here. After a few kilometres of walking along the lake shore and up onto the road where the lake was inaccessible, he turned back.

He picked up his ringing phone and saw a video-call from Brigitte. *'Bonjour, Brigitte.'* Why was she in a hospital room? His heart dropped. 'What's happened?'

'It's all right.' Brigitte laughed. 'We have a surprise for you.' She moved her phone so he could see Gabriel in bed attached to any number of tubes and cables.

'What the…?'

'Hey, Josue, you worry too much. I'm fine.' Gabriel's voice was croaky, like he needed lots of fluid to lubricate his throat.

'He had his surgery today and has come through very well,' Brigitte was saying.

'But it wasn't scheduled till next month.' What was going on? 'I was going to be there with you.'

'An opportunity come up on the surgeon's schedule so I took it,' Gabriel croaked.

'And you're seriously all right?' Josue asked, even though Gabriel did look fine from here. 'You should've called me. I'd have caught the first plane out.'

'He's tired and sore, but otherwise everything went well.' Brigitte continued, 'We won't talk long or he'll fall asleep on you. But we wanted to tell you so you don't have to come home on our behalf.'

The tension exploded. 'I wanted to be there. Don't you understand?' It had been his excuse for leaving. 'I can't stay here.'

'Why ever not?' Gabriel asked. 'I thought you were enjoying New Zealand.'

'I was.'

'What's happened?'

'Nothing.' Everything. He'd screwed up big time. 'I am coming home.'

'Talk. And stop yelling.'

He hadn't known he was. 'I miss you both.'

'That's good because we're visiting you when I'm up and about.'

'Gabriel, you can't travel for a while after surgery.' What if he got ill on the flight?

'Too late.' Brigitte laughed. 'I booked flights for Christmas to come down to New Zealand. Gab wants to do this more than anything and since he's had a scare I have to agree. Do what we can while we can.'

Suddenly Josue felt as though the world was ganging up on him. A job offer. A baby. And now no reason to have to go home. He couldn't take it all in.

'Josue? You haven't answered my question. What's got you in this state?' Gabriel asked.

'I've got into a mess.'

'And you don't know what to do. Time to stand up and be counted, by any chance?' Gabriel knew him too well.

Josue swallowed his anger. These lovely people didn't deserve it any more than Mallory had. 'I've fallen in love. We're having a baby. I've got a job here if I want it.' The words poured out like he had no brakes.

'Wow.' Brigitte laughed. 'That's our Josue. Doesn't do anything in halves.'

Our Josue. It went straight to his heart. These people *were* his family. 'I've never gone for something so huge before.'

'So what's the problem?' Gabriel croaked, reminding Josue he should finish the call. 'Exactly why are you wanting to return to Nice?'

Josue stared at his mentor and saw the strength that had got him through life this far. Saw the love that went with the strength. And he decided. 'I'm not sure. I'd like to take a risk with Mallory, to stay on and settle down.' Now that he'd put it into words he felt relief settle over him. Had he made up his mind to move forward as easily as that? Impossible, surely?

He had been touching on the possibility for the weeks he'd known Mallory. The time to make up his mind had arrived and he couldn't walk away. He didn't want to. He was ready to take on the future and hopefully enjoy it.

Did this mean he could admit his feelings to her? To take a chance on them as a couple? He had to, otherwise he might as well pack his bags and go. But he wasn't going to. He would stay. He really would.

Mallory sat on the couch with her feet tucked under her backside and Shade's head in her lap. Unable to face anyone, she'd called Pete to ask for the rest of the day off and thankfully he'd agreed. She'd lit the fire, made tea and watched a movie, but she had no idea what it had been about.

When Kayla had rung to see if she needed company and that her dad could bring her over in his campervan, she'd turned her down. There was only one person she wanted to be with and he'd gone off on his own to make some calls apparently. But how long could some calls go on for? It had been hours since he'd left her in bed, looking as though he'd had the world's problems on his shoulders.

He didn't promise to come back, Mallory.

No, he didn't, but she could hope he might.

Shade sat up, her nose pointing towards the front door.

'Who is it, girl?'

The dog leapt to the floor and trotted out of the room.

'Mallory, can I come in?'

Josue. Her heart pounded painfully. This was the moment. She could feel it in her blood. Josue was here to tell her he was going home, that he wouldn't take the job or risk a life with her and their child. He'd be thinking he'd let them down. 'I'm in the lounge.' She pressed Off on the TV remote.

'Hey.' Josue came in and straight over to her where he sat on the other end of the couch. 'You all right?'

She nodded, unable to speak for fear of talking gibberish.

He reached for her hands and enclosed them in his warm ones, his thumbs moving back and forth softly on her cold skin. 'I've had a triple whammy these past couple of days.' He was smiling.

She crooked her head to one side. Smiling. That warm-her-toes smile. 'Sometimes it's best to get everything over and done with all at once.'

His smile widened. 'I'm hoping nothing's over and that this is the beginning of everything I've only ever dreamed about.'

Was she hearing him right? 'You'd better talk in words of one syllable.'

'I love you, Mallory Baine.'

That she could understand. 'Truly?' she blurted. 'It was only hours ago you were telling me how this was a shock and how I didn't understand where you were coming from. That your life had been terrible and I couldn't expect to know why you do the things you do.' She paused, drew a breath. 'Okay, so I've exaggerated, but what I did get was that you weren't interested in staying for the long haul.'

'You kind of got all of that right. I'm sorry for hurting you. I know your trust has been broken before. You can trust me. I've made up my mind to move forward, and that's with you and our baby. I want to give this, and you, all of my heart.'

'Oh, Josue.' She blinked but that didn't stop the tears flowing. She'd waited so long for this moment. A man and a baby. Life couldn't get any better.

'With all my heart, I love you.'

Her skin warmed, her heart changed rhythm to light and zippy. 'As I love you, Josue.'

'Yes, just like that.' He held her gaze. 'I'm going to take the job. I'm not going back to Nice at all. Gabriel and Brigitte are coming out here for Christmas.'

'What about his operation?' There's no way Josue would not be with the man who'd done so much for him.

'All done.' He explained what had happened,

and the more he talked the more relaxed he became.

Josue was happy, she realised. 'You're sure about this, aren't you?'

'I am, but there's one more thing.'

Her heart slowed. *Don't make me sad now.* 'Go on,' she whispered.

'Will you marry me? Live with me and raise our child together?'

Mallory flew across the couch onto his lap and wound her arms around him. 'Yes,' she shouted. 'Yes.'

And then they were kissing and pulling back to smile at each other, and the love coming to her through those eyes told her she'd finally got it right and had found the right man to go through life with. She'd found the romance and love her parents had known. 'I love you so much, Josue. I can't believe I found you right here on this couch. It's going with us wherever we live.'

'About that. You need to find a better hiding place for the key. I don't want any other man wandering in and making himself at home here.'

'There's only one Mr Intruder in my life.' And she went back to kissing him.

The early summer sun streamed onto the lodge's deck, highlighting all the beautiful red and pink roses in their planter boxes lining the carpet leading up to the love of Mallory's life standing watching her as she and her mother began the walk from her single life to the beginning of her shared one, followed by Kayla and Maisie in beautiful cream silk gowns.

The smile lighting Josue's face and the love in his eyes melted her inside. Thank goodness for keys in meter boxes, and a dear friend who hadn't made it home that night. Kayla still teased her remorselessly, saying she was owed plenty for bringing them together.

'Who's that man?' Mallory's mother asked. 'He looks handsome.'

'That's Josue, Mum. I'm marrying him in a minute. Isn't he gorgeous?'

'Yes, darling, he's a stunner. Have I met him?'

Flip-flop went her heart. But she wasn't going to let her mother's condition spoil anything today, and she was determined her mum would have a good time, whether she remembered it or not. 'Yes, you have. He came and asked you if you'd let me marry him.'

'What did I say?'

'When you learned he was from France you said yes, and he hugged you.'

'That's him? Now I remember.'

Some of it anyway. Or maybe Mum was making up bits and pieces. It didn't matter. She was smiling and there was a twinkle in her faded blue eyes. Mallory squeezed her hand tight. 'Love you, Mum.'

They reached the group waiting at the end of their walk and paused. She looked into Josue's eyes and let go of the breath she'd been holding all the way down the aisle. He was here and he looked full to brimming with love for her. This was really happening; it wasn't a dream she was about to wake up from. Josue was real, was the love of her life, and this time she had got it right. Now she understood why she'd stuffed up with the first two men in her life. They had never been the right ones. Josue had always been meant to come along and take away her heart, giving her his in its place.

'Sweetheart, you look beautiful.' Josue leaned in and kissed both her cheeks. 'Stunning.'

Her eyes filled and she couldn't get a word out around the lump in her throat. *I love you.*

He nodded, looked at her mother, gave her two small kisses on her cheeks too. 'Hello, Dorothy. You look lovely, too.'

'I keep telling Mallory Frenchmen kiss like the devil.'

Laughter erupted amongst the seated guests as Maisie took Dorothy by the arm and held her beside Mallory.

Next to Josue, Gabriel and Brigitte laughed

too. They were standing up with him, Gabriel's chest pushed out with pride. 'This is the most special day of my life, Mallory.'

Beside him Brigitte cleared her throat, and winked. 'Second most special.'

'Yes, of course.'

The marriage celebrant took over the proceedings. 'Shall we get the ceremony under way?'

'Yes, let's.' Mallory slid her free hand into Josue's and leaned close. 'I'm done waiting.'

'I can't believe I'm here marrying the love of my life.' Josue pinched his skin. *Oui*, it was true. His heart had been blocking his throat from the moment he'd seen Mallory begin walking up the aisle towards him. Bringing him love and happiness, with their baby warm inside her. He'd never have believed that day he'd boarded the plane to fly to New Zealand that everything was going to turn around for him, and that he'd find the most wonderful woman to share his life with.

Gabriel leaned close, said quietly, 'This is real, Josue.'

The man knew him too well. *'Je sais.'* Right from the bottom of his heart he understood how real and true it was and he couldn't wait to marry Mallory and begin the next phase of their life together.

Breathing deeply, he stood tall and listened to the celebrant begin the ceremony. It went by so fast. He was placing the ring on Mallory's slender finger and feeling the band of love she slipped onto his, and kissing her and hearing Gabriel saying that was enough, all before he knew it. When he heard the celebrant declare them man and wife, Monsieur and Madame Bisset, he lifted Mallory up into his arms and kissed her again. *'Je t'aime.'*

'I love you too,' she said through the kiss.

Dorothy's excited voice cut through their kiss. 'See, I warned you Frenchmen kiss like the devil.' His mother-in-law was a bit of a character despite her health.

Mallory stood against him as he held her around the waist. 'I am so happy it's unbelievable.'

'Non, Mallory. It's believable. It's real. We just got married.'

Maisie handed her back the bouquet Mallory had relinquished to exchange wedding rings. 'I'm so happy. It's about time one of us was married.'

Mallory laughed. 'I think you two should have another shot at getting hitched again.'

Kayla smiled. 'Not me. Not yet. I'm coming right, but I'd like time to get settled back in Queenstown before I even think of men and marriage.' She grinned at Maisie. 'Guess that means you're next.'

'Don't even think you can start hooking me up for dates with every male who lands a ride in your ambulance. I am so not interested.' Maisie shrugged her shoulders, but her gaze had wandered out to the groups of friends standing talking and sipping the champagne that was being handed round.

Josue couldn't figure out who she paused on, but he did notice the sudden intake of breath. So there *was* someone she was interested in.

Mallory whispered, 'Watch this.' Suddenly she tossed her bouquet directly at Kayla who had no choice but to catch it.

Kayla glared at the bouquet, and then at Mallory. 'No, thanks.'

She went to hand it back to Mallory, but her friend laughed and held Josue's hands tight. 'Sorry, but my hands are full.'

'Mallory Baine, I swear you are a sneaky piece of work.'

Josue locked eyes with her. 'Kayla, haven't I introduced you to Mallory Bisset yet?' He loved the sound of his wife's name. He spun Mallory up into his arms and kissed her and kissed her some more. 'I promise to kiss you like the devil when you wake in the morning and before you go to sleep at night.' He leaned closer and whispered, 'And to love you forever.' It wouldn't be hard to do. His heart was in her hands now. Safe.

* * * * *

*If you enjoyed this story, check
out these other great reads from
Sue MacKay*

The GP's Secret Baby Wish
The Nurse's Secret
Reclaiming Her Army Doc Husband
A Fling to Steal Her Heart

All available now!